MW01710208

THE EDGE OF OBSESSION

BLACK OPS CONFIDENTIAL

DIANA MUÑOZ STEWART

The Edge of Obsession, copyright 2019, Diana Muñoz Stewart
Published by Diana Muñoz Stewart
Cover by Richard Lamb
Layout: www.formatting4U.com

Dedicated to my darling husband.
For his patience, love, and support.

Books by Diana Muñoz Stewart

I AM JUSTICE (Black Ops Confidential Book 1)
THE PRICE OF GRACE (Black Ops Confidential Book 2)
THE COST OF HONOR (Black Ops Confidential Book 3)

Chapter 1

"Excuse me, Sister Angelica, I... I..." Stupendous, she not only looked like Maria in *The Sound of Music*—black habit, white tunic, suitcase at her feet—she was stumbling over an apology. "I didn't mean to suggest these habits aren't—"

This was not like her. In the ten or so years that Dada Parish had been going undercover on vigilante ops, she'd taken on dozens of false identities: wealthy Nigerian heiress, international model, security guard, translator, Special Envoy to the UN, to name a few. Leaving behind her real identity as Dada Parish and taking on another was as easy as putting on a coat.

Or had been.

Her palm on her cane, Sister Angelica fanned her fingers. "No apology necessary. If I took affront at every little thing, Sister Dee, I'd be a piss-poor servant of God. Besides, I agree; these habits do belong in a musical."

Piss-poor? Determined not to laugh, Dada smiled at the abbess. The sister in charge of the abbey in Mexico was short, maybe four-feet-eleven, her blue eyes dusty beneath black-rimmed glasses, with silver hair peeking from beneath her habit, and skin as white and dry as talcum powder. If not for their matching outfits, this nun would be Dada's—six feet tall with silky, dark skin—polar opposite. "Thank you, Sister Angelica."

The abbess shook off the thanks. "Stop the men your mother thinks are trafficking women through Mexico. That, more than the money she donated, will be thanks enough."

Dada cringed, horrified she'd voiced the truth about her reconnaissance mission to stop a human trafficking ring. Especially when raised voices funneled around them from the corridor.

Five nuns of diverse backgrounds came from the hallway that led to a stone-lined, courtyard heavy with green plants. They surrounded Dada, greeting her with a mixture of curiosity and eagerness and varying levels of Spanish.

"Hermana Dee, estás aquí." "Sister Dee, you're here."

"Not a moment too soon."

"Serendipity."

"You should come with us."

"Yes, come," the final nun said with the directness of someone who has lived beyond forty. Round face, reddish-tan skin, and a gap-toothed smile, the sister took Dada by the arm and spun her toward the door. "If we don't hurry, we won't be ready for the lunch crowd."

"Lunch crowd?" Dada asked, blinking at the noonday sun as she found herself back on the streets of Oaxaca, a city tightly lined with colorful buildings that surrounded the ancient abbey.

Sister Angelica closed the door with a, "I'll see your bag gets to your room."

Stupendous. Nuns, it turned out, could be a little bossy.

#

Ten minutes after walking into the Benedictine abbey, Dada stood behind the counter at a soup kitchen. Clouds of heat wafted up from the steel food well. Moisture slid from under her habit and along her face. Stifling hat—and she had short hair. What must it be like for the women with longer hair?

Though sweaty, she offered smiles and greetings to the numerous refugees filing along in the cafeteria line. She had no problems communicating with the mostly Spanish speakers.

Languages, she could do. Now, if she could just get this nun thing down.

A man began to play on a worn guitar, and, as the music drifted inside, people took up singing a familiar Mexican lullaby. She hummed along.

With a sudden drop, the music stopped, and like a wave around a sports arena, tension rolled down the line of sisters. They paused serving the food, their heads swinging left.

Dada scanned for what had caused the unease.

Not what.

Who.

Six-feet-something, and that something was fine with a capital F. Wavy auburn hair, sexy trimmed beard, and summer brown eyes. The kind of toned body that a man couldn't hide, even under the long-sleeved over-shirt. Why long sleeves? Was he hiding a conceal-carry? He walked with a slight limp, but in a way that almost looked like a swagger.

Yum. No lie. He was glorious.

And vaguely familiar.

Her heart ratcheted up its pace. Each beat, like a cart ascending on a roller coaster, clicked higher and higher into her throat as this man, this gorgeous swaggering man, made his way toward her.

How did she know him? More importantly, did he know her? If so, would he recognize her? Doubtful. She had on a nun outfit and brown contacts covering her distinct honey-colored eyes. Still…

She brushed the shoulder of the sister next to her. "Who is he?"

The sister's expression soured. "Juan The Forger. Works for traffickers—men aligned with the cartel that owns this area. He donates every week—"she nodded toward the donation boxes dotting the room—"then takes a tray for an older woman in town who can't leave her home."

"So he's a nice devil?"

Scooping rice for the next-in-line, she said, "What's worse—a man who does bad with no concept of right and wrong, or a man who does bad, *allows* bad, because he benefits from it? And then, to assuage his guilt, donates?"

Dada knew the answer to that. In a flash, she was nine again, held prisoner in a room while one man, a very rich French man, raped her. He'd brought her many gifts over her four years of captivity. Taught her. Spoke kindly to her. But that was to assuage his guilt. And none of it made up for the pain, humiliation, and fear he'd caused her.

Dada slapped down her attraction to the man walking toward her. Slapped it down and put it in chains. Chains as heavy as the loss symbolized by the woven leather bracelet she wore as a talisman. She grasped the familiar band.

After accepting a scoop of yellow rice, the man stopped in front of Dada and his eyes widened.

Her heart plunged. He *did* recognize her. He did.

Heat spiked in her body. A knowing warmth and an unexpected, and unwelcome thought... *It's him. Him.*

Him who? Dada shook herself. *Blink. Must blink.* Not easy when those dare-me-to brown eyes, framed in a bounty of lashes, locked on her.

Beside her, the sister said, "Do you want beans or are you filling your belly looking at Sister Dee?"

His pale skin flushed. *"Disculpe, Hermana. Frijoles, por favor."* "Excuse me, Sister. Beans, please."

His Spanish was good, but accented. A British accent, Welsh specifically. That was it! That was how she knew him.

The memory of a sleek young man driving down the pitch with a soccer ball surfaced. The surge of admiration and longing. Her heart in her throat. Her eyes glued to the screen.

She knew him from her love of sport. Specifically, her favorite sport. He was a soccer player. An amazing one. Or… he had been. If she remembered correctly, he'd been injured right before signing a contract for the Premier League—which explained the limp.

He worked for traffickers? And the ones she wanted information from since they owned this area? Lords and ladies, the mighty had fallen.

A flare of excitement lit her chest. The luck that had followed her escape from French Guiana continued. Because of this staggering luck, she'd learned to accept and jump at opportunity. Just as she'd learned to accept and find a way around complications—knowing something would eventually turn in her favor. Too good to be true didn't mean it wasn't true. Not for her.

Not exactly a nun-thing to do, but she could use what she knew of him—his past and his obvious guilt—to pressure him into being her asset. She'd get close to him, exploit his weakness, and ignore the way he made her feel. A minor complication, that.

With her heart still in her throat, she scooped the beans into a small paper cup then handed it to him.

Their fingers brushed. A strong, certain flash of awareness shot up her arm and down her spine. Primitive heat thrummed through her, arousing every gasping nerve. Longing. Need. Surrender.

They made eye contact and she saw the same want reflected in his burning gaze. His mouth curled into a grin. Oh, this could be a big complication.

Noticing, the sister cleared her throat.

With a jolt, he drew back the foil-lined cup. His face reddened and he moved off with a, "Sorry, Sister. Sorry."

No need to ask what he apologized for. It was obvious. One did not make lust-eyes at a nun.

Chapter 2

Making his way around the locals and tourists crowding the sidewalk, Sion envisioned his room in Hell. The Devil was probably preparing his bed right now. *Here, boyo, lie down on this dry straw.* Right smack dab in the middle of hellfire. He'd just... merciful heaven, he needed to have sex. Been too long. What other reason could he give for making googly eyes at a nun?

Googly eyes, mate?

All right. Fine then. Everything else in his life was dishonest, so he could face the truth in his own bloody head. He'd lusted on her hard. Couldn't really help himself. His gaze had traveled the length of her tunic, one that couldn't hide those hips and swells and... Good lord, he was doing it again.

Stop it, you daft bugger. There's a line you need to step away from. Drive away from. Speed away from.

He tried to blink away the heat of his shame and the scorching hot memory of her. Just hadn't expected... skin as silky as the finest sheets. And her stare, so direct. Like she knew him. Like she wanted him. Like... she knew his soul was destined for Hell.

Bugger. And he had to come back here at the end of next week? *Ah, well, something to look forward to.*

Stop it!!

"Hold on, there. Hold on, please."

The whisky voice slid into his stomach and warmed it. That was a good voice. He turned. Bollocks. It was her, jogging down the sidewalk toward him, her breasts bouncing under her—

Nun tunic, you perv.

He stopped staring. His face heated to hellfire levels. At least he'd get accustomed to the heat of his future destination.

She slowed, then pointed at his hands. "I'm sorry. You can't take the tray."

What? He looked down. *Ach y fi*. He'd been so determined to get out of there that he'd forgotten to put the food into the containers and insulated carrier he'd brought. "Sorry, Sister. I'll just transfer the food. I have a sack."

She laughed. "You have a sack, huh?"

What? He stared at her twinkling brown eyes. Had she— What kind of joke was that? What kind of nun was she?

He cleared his throat and his obviously confused mental direction. "Sorry about the tray."

Pursing her lips, she dismissed the issue with a jaunty, "I'm told you do false papers. But other than that, you're honest. A good man. A man willing to bring food to a woman in need."

Humiliating. She thought he worked for the traffickers. As did everyone else around here. Ah, well, there was nothing he could do about it. He'd sacrificed his dignity and a morality he thought unbreakable in his search for Sophia.

With a hand to her chest, she said, "I'm Sister Desdemona. Dee for short. And you're Welsh."

She had a good ear. He balanced the tray and tried to work his sack out from his backpack.

She reached forward. “Let me hold it.”

Hold *what*?

She licked her lips with a pink tongue.

The pinkest tongue he’d ever seen. *Ach-y-fi*, the tray. She meant the tray.

Hellfire, boyo. Think about that.

“Thank you, Sister.”

He swung off his backpack, took out the square insulated container, then transferred the food as she held the tray. When he was done, she slipped the tray under one arm, smiled at him, then threw the coldest of cold water right in his face.

“I saw you play. Before your injury, I mean.”

Fuck. Balls. Fuck. “Not sure what you’re talking about.”

His denial didn’t seem to bother her. Probably used to degenerates lying to her.

“Juan is a form of John,” she said. “And Sion is the Welsh form of John. Your name when you played, soccer... ah, you call it football, was Sion Bradford. Clever.”

Not so clever. She’d picked that apart in two seconds. Tidy. And a sports fan. And hot as hell. And a nun. Shame. “I’m not interested in being that guy, Sister.”

“Dee.”

“Sister Dee.”

“Just Dee.”

There’s a lovely. “I’m not interested in being that guy, Dee.” He lowered his voice. “I *can’t* be that guy. Not here. Do you understand?”

Her eyes turned serious. "In your line of work, I imagine it could be dangerous." She fiddled with the tray. "I'll keep your secret."

She'd spoken English. "You're American?" And unlike her perfect Spanish, with the hint of some other accent under her American accent. "Not what I'd expected."

She gave him another of those sly grins. "Not the first time I've heard that."

No doubt. They stared at each other. God, she was beautiful. And funny. And kind.

Ach. Enough.

"Thanks for your help, luv—uh, Sister. I mean, uh, Dee."

Feeling like an absolute sod, he fled before he could get himself into any more trouble. Glancing back to wave or make things less weird, he found her eyes on his arse.

She caught him catching her. She smiled, shrugged, and said, "I'm a nun. Not dead."

Heat, like exploding fireworks, *pop-pop-pop*ped, shooting through his body. He stumbled.

Bloody. Hell. Fire.

Chapter 3

Through the swirling smoke rising from the joint pinched between his yellow-stained nails, Armand Stoker watched the couple across the street. Shifting on his red plastic chair, he lifted the wet tip to his mouth.

Acrid relief glided down his throat, nestled into his lungs. He bit back his breath as ash floated from the joint to land on and disappear against his pale skin. Even drugs couldn't dilute his rage. It was her, dressed as a nun, talking with Juan the Forger.

A man passing by stopped and blocked his view. "You can't smoke here," the man said, pointing to the restaurant's No-Smoking sign shaded by the restaurant's faded awning.

American, judging by the accent and shoes. If he'd been from around here, he wouldn't have said a word. Not just because Armand had a reputation and an imposing frame, but because all here knew his boss owned this restaurant, and used it to launder money. The locals enjoyed cheap drinks and food.

Giving the American idiot a look that would curl the blood of any beast with sense, a look that goosed the man and sent him shuffling off, he took another drag. Across the street, Dada had turned and walked away with a tray tucked under her arm.

She didn't look his way, but, even if she had, he doubted she would recognize him. Prison had not been kind to him. She bore no scars, but had become a nun. A waste of all that beauty.

A beauty that made him ill. It was as his mother often said, "If there is character, ugliness becomes beauty. If there is none, beauty becomes ugliness."

She should be buried with the child she hadn't even been woman enough to birth. And he should still be in French Guiana, still handsome, having inherited a successful business.

If not for Dada… Bile rose into his dry, smoke-sore throat. His phone buzzed, sliding across the ash-covered plastic table. He winced at the number. Walid.

Grinding out the stub with his fingers, he answered. "Armand here."

"Where is here?" Walid asked. "You're not at the compound, and not where you should be, at my front gate. Do you have somewhere else you need to be?"

Red fury burst through his body, cementing in the molars of his grinding teeth. His mother, the earth surely rotten where she'd been laid to rest, had challenged him in the same demeaning way. If not for the girls and protection Walid provided, he wouldn't put up with it.

He wouldn't need to put up with it much longer.

"I was just headed back to the ranch, Walid. I was in town, seeing to"—he paused to fill his voice with what he hoped Walid understood was repressed disgust—"your entertainers."

There was a longer pause on Walid's end. Armand smiled. The man depended on him to a degree that was not wise. Despite all his cruelty, Walid had never learned to see his own weakness. A grown man who still thought of himself as a little brother.

Walid's raspy voice filled the line again, but with less venom. "The last shipment sent to the Americas, you oversaw it, no?"

A worm of dread twisted in his gut. To be caught stealing from Walid—and more importantly, his older brother Aamir—would earn him a brutal, sadistic death. "I did."

"Our buyer claims a specific item has gone missing. His man in El Salvador had described it, and he'd very much looked forward to receiving it. It never reached him. Do you know what I reference?"

"A missing item?" *Merde*. In all the years he'd been stealing girls from Walid, he'd never been challenged about his thefts. And this one? What had been so special about a plump, doe-eyed girl? "Yes. I'm handling it."

"So you know where it is?"

He knew exactly where she was. How long she'd screamed. How long she'd cried, begged. And where she was buried.

"There was only one item lost in transport. I've men out looking for it. Not to worry."

"I don't want to hear reassurances. Reassurances are something for women and children when you direct them to the gas chamber. I want to know how this happened, where it happened, and who is looking for the item. Come with these answers. Now." Walid ended the call.

Armand stared at his phone, wishing he could reach through time and end the man who had just made his life more difficult. Since that wasn't possible, he called the only number he had memorized.

The person on the other end answered after one ring. “Yes?”

“We need to replace that girl, the doe-eyed one. Start looking among the refugees.”

“I’ll see to it.” The line was uttered with a tone as flat and determined as the man’s personality. A good second-in-command. Together, they’d established a growing side business. Soon, it would be big enough to allow them to get rid of Walid. But not now. Now, was a dangerous time. A time he could ill afford to do what he intended to do.

“I’ll also need your help in covering the disappearance of a nun.”

There was a long moment of silence that Armand understood. The people here were very religious. Taking a refugee was one thing, but taking a nun?

“A nun will be difficult.”

“More difficult than saving your life?”

Another pause. Longer. Heavier. “We’ll have to burn the body.”

Chapter 4

A warm gust molded Dada's tunic against her thighs as she strolled over the cobbled streets of the *zocola*, the main square. Late for the lunch rush, as was becoming her habit—along with nun puns—she hurried past carts of traditional Mexican foods, fruits and vegetables, flowers, and pottery.

Oaxaca was a pleasant city with historic buildings, terra cotta tiled roofs, stone arches, steepled white churches, and an abundant mix of locals, tourists, and refugees.

A *lot* of refugees. She homed in on one, a smiling toddler pulling a wheeled, wooden cockatoo. His mother sat, cup raised, begging for coin.

For a moment, Dada marveled at the tiny jeans covering the boy's little marching legs.

The ache in her heart thickened into her throat. Looking away, her fingers automatically ran along the weave of her worn leather bracelet.

She was an undercover operative in the League of Warrior Women. Rescued from near death, she was here to rescue others, not indulge in what-ifs.

Chastising herself, she glanced one last time at the boy—and saw two men, twenty-somethings, come up fast behind the child. They didn't slow, headed straight for the boy, then knocked him over.

Dada gasped. The boy fell and cried out. The refugee woman got to her feet, barked at the men, lifting her child out of their way as she backed up. The men followed. One of them wearing a green t-shirt spoke harshly, crowding her and the child.

Walking in their direction, Dada heard Green Shirt say, "…rather beg in the street?"

The other young man in a white t-shirt with a Honduran accent said, "Why wouldn't you want a job?"

The young mother, nineteen or so, clutched her son, backing away. "I don't want that. Tell him no."

"Come with us," Green Shirt said, reaching for her. "It's safer."

Fury steamrolled over Dada, propelling her straight into Green Shirt. Her shove sent him lurching, arms spinning. He sprawled to the ground, then darted back to his feet with a quickness that would've been comical if it weren't so startling.

He swung around, teeth bared.

Dada tried to ease the tension. She could not afford to fight these men here where someone might see. "Never let it be said that a nun doesn't know how to get a man's attention."

"Go back to God," Green Shirt hissed, reaching into his pocket.

Dada stepped forward, hampered by the width of her tunic. She snagged the man's wrist. Holding tight, she dragged him forward, twisted, then brought him to his jean-clad knees.

His hand opened. A knife dropped to the ground.

"Leave him go," White Shirt said, moving in on her right side. His frantic eyes locked on her. His shoulders grew tight.

He had something in his hand.

A pipe.

Obviously not a practicing Catholic.

Dada shifted her feet as wide as she could into a balanced fighting stance, putting pressure on the delicate bones in Green Shirt's wrist, bending his hand back. He cried out and swung feebly at her with his other hand.

White Shirt moved in.

Damn it. She'd have to fight.

She dropped Green Shirt's hand, sidestepped, nearly tripped again. This damn tunic.

A figure moved gracefully between her and White Shirt. Huge biceps, veined forearms, broad shoulders, and a half-sleeve tattoo full of colors.

In a boxer's stance, Sion ducked the whoosh of White Shirt's swinging pipe. He came up under it, sent a devastating blow into White Shirt's face. The *thunk* made her cringe.

White Shirt's head snapped back. Blood rolled down from his nose and from the split skin above it. Pinning his glare on Sion, White Shirt swung again.

Dada had a second to react as Green Shirt rose to his feet and charged at Sion from behind.

Grabbing her tunic, Dada freed her legs, kicked the back of Green Shirt's kneecap.

He fell, dropping to his shoulder, rolled, but then was back up, springing at her.

Dada's brain shifted to attack. Her hands came up.

Green Shirt screamed. Put a hand to his ear. Swung around.

Knuckles bloody, Sion sent another strike at the man's head. It barely skimmed as the guy moved quickly. They circled each other, avoiding White Shirt on the ground, a bleeding mess.

Sion delivered a series of blindingly quick boxing blows to Green Shirt. He grunted as the first two hits landed, dodged the last strikes, backed up, then looked toward his knife.

"Don't," Sion said, his tone ice.

A whistle sounded from across the square.

Police.

Green Shirt jolted into action, dropping his hands, and running over to his friend. He dragged White Shirt until he could get up and run.

The officer who'd blown his whistle ran across the square, waving people who'd gathered to watch the fight out of his way. He gave chase, telling Sion as he passed to, "Get them to safety."

There was a moment of settling tension, as everyone realized the fight was over. People drifted off. Some looked away. Some offered Sion praise.

Dada quickly bent down and pocketed Green Shirt's knife. She then picked up the child's toy, then brought it to him.

He hid his face in his mother's shoulder, so it took a couple of moments to get his attention. But his dark eyes eventually moved up and then to the toy. Dada encouraged him to take it. He did, wrapping chubby fingers around it, hugging it to his chest. His mother kissed away his tears.

"Thank you," the woman said to her and then to Sion, who had bent to pick up his flannel shirt. She understood now why he always wore it—his tattoo was a footballer kicking into a goal.

Her gaze traveled from the tattoo over his broad

chest, and she smiled. “Yes. Thanks for your help. I wouldn’t have wanted to release my jiu jitsu on them.”

Knuckles bloody, sweat soaking his shirt, a smile as pure and clean as sunlight cracked his face. He gave a long, low laugh. The sound raced along her body, settling warmth in her stomach. “Sister—”

“Dee.”

“Dee. Certainly can’t have martial arts nuns breaking assailants in half. Wouldn’t be proper.”

“No,” she acknowledged. “It would start rumors and keep people up all night with worry.”

Eyes still dancing, he said, “*Ah*, if they’re anything like me, they already have a hard time sleeping since you arrived.”

Their gazes held. His playful brown eyes smoldered. Dada wanted to reach out and touch him.

“Excuse me, Sister,” the toddler’s mother said, causing both her and Sion to jump.

Caught flirting with a Welshman when she was undercover as a nun. Not her finest hour.

Chapter 5

He was a heathen. It was practically written on stone tablets near a burning bush. He was corrupted enough to flirt with a woman of God. And to want to do much more than that, God save him.

He watched as Sister Dee introduced the two of them to the refugee woman. The woman, practically a girl, introduced herself as Rosa and her tear-stained child as Carlos.

Though Dee hadn't asked, Rosa murmured, "I have never begged before. When I lived in Honduras, I had a food cart. But things there became so bad..." She looked at her son, slung on one hip, clutching his toy. "The gangs, the bosses could own you and your life with a look. Needing to keep my son safe, I sold my cart for this journey. Yesterday, I had my bag with all my money stolen, so now, I can't even afford a place for us. And there are people here just as bad as those we fled."

"Who is just as bad?" Dee said. "The men who left here?"

Rosa shook her head. "Those men are headed north like me. They were paid by another man. He said he wished to give me a job. The men he hired to offer me the job, said he promised there would be no sex." She rolled her eyes. "But I've heard stories of other women who have taken these jobs and never come back."

A gnawing suspicion started in Sion's gut. There was no person more vulnerable than someone desperate for money. Add onto that threats to her son, and it was a wonder she'd had the guts to stand up to them.

Rosa hitched Carlos up on her hip. "This was the second time I've been asked. I was worried it was traffickers, and that someone might try to take me."

"Not so sure about that," Sion said. "This is settled territory."

Dee frowned. "Meaning?"

"An uneasy truce exists here between traffickers and the police. Traffickers don't steal women in the area, making more trouble for police already overtaxed with the drug cartels. The police look the other way when women from outside are moved through here."

Dee's eyebrows drew in. Her lips thinned out, grew tight.

Bugger, he pulled at his beard. In all the time he'd been working to get in with Walid to find Sophia, and ultimately expose the trafficking routes, he'd never wanted to tell anyone the truth before.

Dee put a palm on Rosa's shoulder. "If what Sion said is correct, you should talk to the police about—"

"No. Please, Sister," Rosa said, shaking her head. "Some of the police can't be trusted. I don't want trouble. I just want to get to safety." She met Dee's eyes. "You understand?"

"Okay," Dee said. "But you must let me put you up at the hotel. At least, until I can find a way to help you on your journey."

Rosa looked more afraid than grateful. "I can't let you pay my room—"

With a soft sigh and a softer look, Dee said,

"Please, dear one, it is my honor to help you. It is the work of my Lord. And His work I will always seek opportunity to fill."

Sion glanced down at his worn trainers. Dee was a good woman. A woman who faced down rich jerks, helped refugees, and kept his secret. Just made him want her more.

Rosa relented, and Dee bent to the little boy, Carlos, and said, "You are courage and light and one of God's precious children. Don't let anyone ever make you feel small."

He felt that in his gut. Looked like God got all the best women. Couldn't really fault Him for it.

After Dee straightened, they made their way across the square to the hotel. Dee went inside to secure the room and Sion saw his opportunity.

He leaned down to Rosa, trying not to let his size intimidate. "Take this money and my card. I want to help you get someplace safe."

"Why would you help me in this way?"

"Because I've seen what happens when a particular woman catches the eye of a man with power."

The memory slammed into him.

Gunshots from outside sent the students scrambling from the crates that served as stools, diving for the dirt. Easels and carefully made paintings went over.

"Down, down," Sion told his art students, though his warning had been unnecessary. The children in the El Salvador village knew the score and had already dropped.

Except Sophia, protected by her father in so many ways. She had frozen on her seat. Sion had grabbed her, brought her to the ground as shouts and screams had flowed through the metal grated window.

And the warning from Sophia's father, waiting outside for his pequeña artista, little artist. "Run, Sophia!"

Sophia screamed, "Papi!"

Five men burst inside. The first man's eyes fell on Sophia. "Niña, ven conmigo." Girl, come with me.

Lurching to his feet, Sion had shoved Sophia toward the back exit where the other students had fled. The man who'd spoken rushed to grab her.

Sion's fist had connected with the man's head.

Five against one. Unlike today, that fight, he'd lost.

Rosa hesitated, staring at the card.

He urged. "Please. It's just a phone number. You call. I help. No strings. Promise."

Another second of hesitation, and she took the card.

He hoped she called. If she needed a way out, he would help her. That's what he did in his spare time. It helped ease the guilt of what he'd done to get in with Walid in order to find Sophia. A child he'd let down in the worst way possible.

He played with Carlos until Sister Dee returned with the room key. Rosa took Carlos inside, gushing once more to Dee, grateful in a way that Dee seemed genuinely uncomfortable with.

Sion found his heart filling with a warmth that sent terror through his body. Lust was one thing, but genuine affection…

After Rosa disappeared into the hotel, Dee turned to him. "Would my hero care to walk me to the soup kitchen?"

Hero? Pain stabbed him in the chest. He badly wanted her to see him as a hero. Not as the guy who worked for slavers. "Oh, aye. But I probably protected those blokes from you more than you from them."

She laughed, and they moved off. Leg screaming in pain after his fight, he limped more noticeably. After a few uncomfortable steps, she gestured at his leg. "I recall reading about your injury. It was a bar fight, right?"

He glanced away. Cringed. A bar fight? That's how people remembered it. And for most people he wouldn't care. But her? "Do I look like the type to throw away my career on booze and anger?"

"So what happened?" Though his tone had been hot, she didn't return the frustration.

They passed trinket-sellers, food stalls, and people eating lunch by the fountain. It was a beautiful day, but his head filled with ugly memories. Learning to walk again. Using drugs and alcohol to numb the pain. The long torturous road to mental and physical recovery. "Too nice a day to get into all that."

"I could google it."

Bloody hell. She didn't hold back. She didn't hold herself even above her own curiosity. "Didn't think you knew about google blackmail, *Sister*."

Her gaze swung to him, held him in a direct and sure stare. "I'm a nun. I don't live on another planet."

He broke eye contact, and rubbed at the knot of pain forming at the top of his bum leg. Truth was, he wanted her to know the what had happened.

After a beat of silence, he relented to his own desire to be seen and known by her as a man other than the one who did false papers for slavers. "I had an exhibition game in the States, then went out afterward to blow off steam. As I was leaving the bar, one of my mates, a guy known to have a temper, along with a morality problem, was dragging a woman into his truck. Not a stretch to guess his intent. I ran over, punched him in the side, and tossed him to the ground. I was taking her inside to call the authorities, and—"

She made a sound, as if the memory had just come back to her. "He shot you in the leg three times."

"Aye." That he'd been shot in the leg three times the papers had gotten right. "Bloke who'd done it claimed self-defense. He wasn't prosecuted."

Sion lost full use of his leg, his contract, but the man—the one who'd been about to kidnap and rape an innocent woman—had lost nothing. He'd even gone on to have a magnificent career—only to revert to form. Years later, he was arrested for trying to rape a different woman.

Dada nodded her head. "The woman refused to testify."

"He'd paid her off."

"And the papers began to spin a different story. You went after him in a drunken rage. Him shooting you was self-defense."

"Had to spin it that way or the squad would've lost two star players."

She reached out to him, grabbed his hand, and squeezed. "They didn't have to. Just because they would have lost games or money was no reason to lose their morals. You deserved better."

The warmth of her skin against his flooded through his body, even as a knot of emotion fisted in his throat.

He gently pulled his hand away. It was that or plead with her to leave the church for him, tell her that he'd lost his morals, and that she should join him on the dark side.

Clenching and unclenching his damp hands, he said, "Next time we talk, I want to hear about you. About how you came to be a nun. Deal?"

A troubled expression crossed her beautiful face. "That story would be filled with more errors than those articles written about you."

And with that bit of makes-you-wonder, she turned and walked toward the soup kitchen.

Chapter 6

Seated on the floor of her sparse room at the convent, Dada waved her wrist—chipped under her skin with a security device and GPS tracker—over her laptop. It beeped.

She opened her laptop and entered a secret site on the dark web. It was empty. For a moment, she stared at a blue screen, but then there was a beep. A box appeared and, inside it, was a sharply angled, red-brown face.

Dark eyes twinkling, her sister Justice began to laugh. “Do they make you wear that fucking hat in your sleep? The shower?”

Dada clicked her teeth together. She’d gotten so used to the habit that she’d forgotten she had it on. “Laugh all you want, abrasive one. I’m doing all of this for your mission.”

“Testy,” Justice said, still laughing. “It’s the celibacy, isn’t it?”

Another box appeared. Gracie. The part in her red hair visible as she focused on one of the many other computer screens in her office.

“Hey, all,” Gracie said, looking up at her central monitor. Her green eyes widened. Her hand came up, covering her laughter.

Joyous news. This was the way her night was going to go.

Tony popped on a split second later, his hazel eyes focused on the screen. His instant laughter boomed over her. "D," he said, wiping at the tears running down his face. "You'se found it. The one cover ya can't pull off."

He continued to lose it. Dada ground her teeth as the edges of her own mouth began to give way.

She loved these disrespectful people. The League of Warrior Women was, in large part, made up of the adopted members of the Parish family—twenty-six females and two males. When adopted into the family—twenty-eight kids and growing—she'd been assigned a unit. These were the siblings she'd trained with, confided in, fought with, ran operations with as an undercover agent.

"Would you all like time to get yourselves together? I can go get some tea and come back."

Slowly, they settled down. Then each of the boxes shuffled right as another box opened. Bridget's hair was a nest of strands stabbed with a comb on the side of her head. Her brown eyes appeared sleepy under her glasses. She blinked, leaned closer. A small smile lit her face. "I like your hat."

All four of her siblings burst into laughter. It took a few more minutes of patience, patience that surely earned her sainthood, before they calmed down enough to get down to business.

When they did, she gave them an overview of what had happened since coming to Mexico, including her new contact. Except, because she'd promised him, she kept Juan's true identity to herself. She did, however, tell them what he'd told her with Rosa. This was important. Someone was taking women from the town.

"So this woman in the square," Tony said, causing the frame around his box to light up, "someone offered her a job, and she said other women had accepted the jobs and disappeared? Isn't that what the cartels do?"

"Yes," Dada said, "but, as I explained, Juan claims this isn't what's happening here. He says this is settled territory."

"But this Juan guy," Justice said, "works for Walid, so maybe he's lying."

Justice's voice said her patience was on a razor's edge. Pretty much where Justice's patience started and ended, but especially with this mission. A mission to take down the men who had killed Justice's biological sister.

"I believe he was telling me the truth," Dada said. "It makes sense."

"Well, fuck," Justice said, "if it has nothing to do with Walid, it'll have to wait until this op is over. We can't risk discovery right now, and you poking around asking questions about missing women is a time bomb."

"Asking questions is why I'm here. I can do both. Find out about Walid's security, the people around him, and research what is happening to these women."

"We don't only need information on Walid. We need his routes," Justice said. "Specifics on how women are being secreted across North America. We need to stop the flow—"

Dada switched her gaze to Tony. "I'm mentioning it so the team leader can make the call."

Tony cleared his throat. Justice jumped in and over him. "I wish the League could take on every case, but there are rules. A process. Focus on the case in front of you. The approved one."

"Even if women are being lured away?" Dada asked, ready to fight for Rosa and women like her.

"Settle down," Tony interrupted. He rubbed at his face. "Right now, it's a no-brainer. Finding info on one situation most likely will find info on the other. This Juan guy is key. Get in front of him every chance you can. Expose some part of you, feed him some truth, so he's more likely to trust you."

Expose herself? Feed him? *Yes. Please.* Heat rose from her fluttering belly to her face. Thanks to the sun god's gift of melatonin, no one could see the heat flushing her face.

"You okay? Looking a little distracted," Tony said.

Uh. Tony. Stop being so observant.

"Leave Dada alone," Bridget said. "It's hard enough being on assignment, having women disappearing around you while researching a trafficker's business without getting teased."

God bless Bridget. Still, her siblings wouldn't be put off with an admonishment. They were evaluating her now. Closely. Which meant they required an answer. And what had Tony just said about giving some truth? She sighed. "Juan is cute, all. Very cute."

"Uh oh," Gracie said. "Stay clear of any complications. You know how that turns out for this family."

She did. Well, she knew how badly it had turned out for Gracie.

“Not to worry,” she told her siblings, comfortable now that she’d distracted them from asking deeper questions. “I’m not interested in any man who would be party to those who would enslave a woman. And you all have to recognize the truth of that.”

There was a beat of silence. A recognition of her pain. And acceptance of her answer. All here had been rescued in one way or another. All here had given their lives to the League in place of any life that could be outside the League of Warrior Women. And that made them one, connected in a way that no one would ever be able to come between.

Chapter 7

The street on which Dada found Sion's apartment was shadowed and rundown—the exact place one would expect to find a forger who worked for sex-traffickers. Now, to see exactly what Sion Bradford a.k.a Juan was doing.

Covering a yawn, Dada entered the building. Nun hours sucked. Four a.m. prayers? Five- thirty breakfast? And that was just the start of the grueling day. Why had Momma thought this would be a good cover for her?

This area had so much to offer, museums, mole, fabulous restaurants, mezcal, clubs, glorious ruins. But not for her. If she hadn't found a way to bend the rules, she'd have spent all her time praying.

Inside the cool, dimly lit corridor, she knocked on a pitted door marked, "*Gerente*." Manager.

The door swung open and Dada looked down at an elderly Mexican woman with silver hair and brown eyes, sitting in a wheelchair.

"Hello. My name is Sister Dee. Juan said you might be in need. I came to check on you."

And to find out what she knew about Juan.

Hearing Juan's name brought a smile to the woman's lips. She introduced herself as Yolanda.

Yolanda then pushed her chair backward and beckoned Dada inside to the kitchen. She took a seat at the glass topped table.

As she made tea, Yolanda talked about Juan. He was such a good boy. So kind.

Dada didn't point out that he wasn't a boy. He was all man. Or that he worked for human traffickers. "How nice to have him here. You must get lonely."

Yolanda shook her head. "I'm not alone. My son is here."

"Your son?"

"That's me," a man said, stepping out from a door in the kitchen, through which she saw a bedroom. He wore blue coveralls. The name on his pocket read Geraldo.

"*Que es esto*?" Geraldo said.

"What is this?" A little rude, Geraldo. And a bit young to be this woman's son. He couldn't be older than twenty-four. He had direct blue eyes and a skin tone halfway between Yolanda's dark one and some unknown lighter-skinned parent.

Yolanda gently told her son, "Sister is here checking on me."

Geraldo blinked and did a double take. His eyes widened. "Sorry, Sister. I didn't see..."

He trailed off. They stared at each other. He hadn't noticed she was a nun? She was wearing the full getup, habit and all. "It's quite all right, my child," she said.

He dragged his hand up and down the front of his chest and spoke slowly, as if he had to search a moment for each word, "I'm to fix the pipes in 4C."

He walked out without another word. Hmmm. Could be Geraldo's brain worked differently?

Yolanda watched her son go, her eyes filled with love. She pointed to him. "Another good boy."

A flash of pain for this woman and her son lanced her heart. Sion seemed like a good man, but he was involved with some very bad people. She hoped trouble didn't follow Sion here.

After a few more moments asking questions about *Juan*, including which apartment was his, Dada excused herself with a promise to return.

#

The unfortunate consequence of breaking into someone's apartment to discover things you wished to know was that you could discover things that truly surprised you.

Sion's one-room apartment had bags of stolen passports from all over the world. They were stacked on a wooden drafting table, spread across his unmade bed, deposited on the breakfast bar by the kitchenette. Along with the passports was the technical equipment to alter them—multiple tools for cutting and pasting, printing machines, blue lights, and lighted magnifying lenses. And all of that was more or less expected. What was unexpected was the paint supplies and paintings that lay near and on an easel. They were heartbreakingly beautiful. She hadn't known he painted.

And even more surprising...

She lifted the Canadian passport and stared at the woman. Maria Salazar Montalvo the passport read. The picture on the passport was Rosa, the young woman from the square.

She scanned the open and drying passports, hanging from a wire like a mini-clothesline strung over the desk, and spotted another familiar face. Rosa's son. Sion had made a passport for him, too. And there were others. Men and women she'd seen at the soup kitchen.

Sion was making false passports to get Central American refugees out of Mexico into safer countries. At one of the printers, she picked up a stack of plane tickets for destinations all over the world, not just the U.S. and Canada.

"Sister?"

Dada jumped a mile. Swinging around, she dropped the passports. Sion squatted on the fire escape, staring at her through the window, his mouth set in a firm, disappointed line.

She brought a hand to her chest. "You scared the life out of me."

He climbed into the window. "Sorry about that."

Hard to miss his sarcasm.

"Don't usually have guests break into my flat. Not sure of the protocols."

Dada shook her head. "I didn't break in. The apartment was..."

She trailed off. The apartment couldn't have been unlocked if he'd left from the fire escape. And, apparently, he had. She turned back to the door, scanned until she spotted the small, nearly invisible device that had registered her entrance. No wonder she'd missed it.

That was very high tech. Hmmm. He used his money for the oddest things. Judging by this room, not really to enrich himself. A gorgeous forger with a big heart. There was definitely more here than met the eye.

She turned back around, smiling. "I need your help."

Shaking his head, Sion swallowed the distance between them with his sexy swaggering gate. "You broke into my flat because you need my help?"

Silent, he stopped feet from her. She had to crane her neck, which was rare—and uncomfortable—for her. She often thought an unconscious reason women wore heels was to have the advantage of looking a man in the eyes. It made sense. At least to her. Height gave her a better sense of control and situational awareness.

Not having that advantage made her supremely uncomfortable. Not only that, but the heat he directed at her rolled forward like lava, enveloping her senses. Parts of her body tingled, moistened. Her mouth for one. And lower.

He stared down at her with those give-me-a-sign brown eyes. "Want to try again, luv?"

Seemed wrong to lie to eyes that beautiful. Maybe lying wasn't the way to go. No way to deny what he did to her, how his physical presence made her feel. Gooey. "Help might be the wrong word." She licked her lips. "I felt a strong need to be near you. With you."

Feminists everywhere would be cringing at her using her sexuality to get out of this situation. And, internally, so was she. Well, a little.

He was so very hot.

"Really," he smirked, leaned closer. "Is that how you intend to play this?"

He had a right to doubt her. And she had a right to make his doubts disappear. Quick as a hot second, she fisted his shirt and pulled him to her. Her lips took his, eager and hungry and wild and so very happy to finally, finally be kissing him.

For a breathless moment, his lips were still against hers. But then he moaned. His tongue pushed into her mouth, played against hers. A bare moment of heat and naked desire raked painfully through every cell in her body.

A flash, a millisecond of surrender. So good. She had not felt heat like this... desire like this... well, ever.

Sion jumped back, leaving her breathless and hot and wet. He began to pace the room. "Oh, fuck. Sister. Sorry, I'm... I just can't..." After a few moments, he turned to her. "You're not a nun. You don't kiss like a nun. Tell me the truth. I need to hear it."

As modern a woman as she was, the idea that he would be so consumed with the desire between them that he would cross that line thrilled her.

But also, seeing his genuine pain and shame, she felt guilt and unease. Such was the life of an undercover agent.

Licking the taste of him, as sweet as any dessert, from her lips, she shook her head. "I can't absolve you or your sins. If that's what you're asking"

He angled his head. "I can't believe you're a nun."

"What do you mean?" She could usually disappear into a role. Was she losing her touch? Or was it that hard for her to play a woman of God? "Why not?"

They stared for a beat. Two. He looked away. "Other than you breaking into people's flats to ask for…" He gave a one-shouldered shrug. "It's, you know." He waved at her.

"Clarify, please."

Desire was back, filling his eyes. And she could see how hard he was against his jeans.

"If you make me say it—"

"Say it."

"Surely, Dee, you've had men stare at you. You must've had people tell you. Surely, you realize how…"

People stared at her. Yes. But she had no idea what people saw when they looked at her.
Unless it seemed a danger, she had no time to waste on looks. "Are you suggesting I'm too beautiful to be a nun?"

That was insulting. She was insulted for nuns everywhere.

"Yes. No. I'm… It's not your beauty alone. It's…. You give off a vibe, an energy."

A vibe? She was giving off a non-nun vibe? Come on. That wasn't her doing. "If my vibe isn't pious enough, doesn't that have more to do with the un-pious inner workings of your own mind?"

"I didn't break into your flat, rifle through your things, and then give you the hottest kiss of your life. It's not me who has a piety issue. So let's try again. Why are you here?"

Chapter 8

Standing in a room full of illegal documents passed to him by his mum, challenging a nun after a kiss that had him as hard as he was confused wasn't how Sion had thought this day would go.

"I told you why I came."

"Right. Sure." He strolled back to her. "Looking for a tumble? Okay. I'm your guy." Let's see what she did with that.

Her eyes widened and then traveled the length of him. For a moment, he thought he'd have to put his mouth where her honey was and found he liked that idea. A lot. But she looked away, down, then grasped the bracelet on her wrist. Bugger. Just as he'd feared, she'd broken in for another reason.

Her posture shifted so she stood with one hip slightly out. "You've made no secret that you create documents for Walid Grimale. I came here looking for leverage. A way to blackmail you into helping Rosa, but I see now..." She motioned around the room. "Why are you helping her and these others? Guilt?"

Guilt didn't cover it. He felt sick to his stomach every time he was asked to create a false identity for Walid or one of his goons. But he'd spent six months creating a relationship with Armand, getting his mum to use her contacts to send him passports, in the hopes of finding Sophia. He scrubbed a hand across his face. "Why would a man help people fleeing a desperate situation find safety? Seems obvious to me."

Her eyebrows drew in. "But this is at odds with what your boss does. He takes advantage of the turmoil in those areas, no? You do know that that is where many of these women trafficked through here come from? Some are coerced, tricked. Others are taken. Can you even imagine the reality?"

A lump erupted in his throat as he tightened his jaw. He didn't need to imagine. He remembered. "So this is about Rosa? You broke into my apartment, kissed me, admitted to wanting to blackmail me all to help Rosa. I don't believe you. Try again."

She exhaled a sound like surrender. "It's not just Rosa. I was hoping to use you as an asset."

That sounded ominous. "Who do you work for?"

Although her eyes never strayed from his face, she grasped that leather bracelet again. Odd. And the only bit of jewelry she seemed to wear.

"I'm an undercover agent, part of the U.S. Catholic Working Group on Global Compacts on Refugees and Migration. The sisters here reached out for assistance. They're worried about the refugees passing through here. As the woman said yesterday, some have gone missing. We are looking to discover how and put a halt to this."

Sion's brow furrowed. "You're a spy? Sent by the Church to investigate the abuse of refugees?" Wasn't the Church a bit more patriarchal than that? "I find it hard to believe they'd send a woman."

Her shoulders straightened. "The Church has a

long and deep history of helping refugees globally. And if you doubt that nuns have a hand in that, that we do the difficult work, you need to go back and educate yourself about us."

She was probably right about that. He knew next to nothing about nuns. But his instinct… *Can't rely on your instinct here, mate. Not when you get tingly every time you look at her.*

Right. His judgment was clouded.

"Okay, Sister. Not sure I believe you." He waved a hand to stop her protest. "Don't take offense. Not sure I believe in God either, but if it is true, I can tell you that your people are better off issuing proclamations from Rome. Being on the ground here, getting involved in this, is dangerous. Way above your pay grade."

Did they pay nuns?

Unperturbed and unruffled by his comments, Sister Dee looked around the room. She scanned his paintings. Her eyes rested on the easel. A painting he'd started the day he'd met her. A dark-skinned woman stood naked on the beach. Her arms thrown to the sky. Streaks of sunlight danced over her, falling as if from heaven. He thought she'd ask about it, prayed she didn't, and nearly sighed aloud when her eyes drifted over to the boxes.

"Where do you get these passports? They're from all over the world. Some don't even have stamps from Mexico, so you're not stealing them from here."

She was back on the offensive. A clever lady. He retrieved the passport she'd dropped. The one for Carlos. He brushed it off. "I think you should leave."

Her gaze dropped to the passport. She nodded at

it. "You're worried about Rosa. But she is safe at a hotel, and there are many others like her. Women your boss takes advantage of. Won't you help me?"

Bugger. Couldn't afford to get tangled with amateurs. Or liars. And, yet, he did have a lot of information. Information he'd intended to turn over to the proper authorities after he'd found Sophia. "What do you want from me?"

For a moment, she seemed taken aback. "Insights into Walid's business, his personal habits, and routes you might be aware of, ways of secreting people through the country."

Information he had. "All right, luv, give me a few days to research you, your explanation, and make a decision."

"But do you have the routes? Telling me now could save lives."

Pushy. "I'm asking for time."

"For what? To go back and tell Walid about me?"

Anger flared. He'd given her enough to show that wasn't true. She was trying to draw him in, maneuver him so that he would tell her something, exposing himself, and aligning with her no matter what. "I don't like where this is going."

"You? And I'm supposed to just accept that you'll keep my secret?"

He took her by the arm, spinning her around, then led her to the front door, opened it, and pushed her through. "Bloody hell. You kept my secret, so trust me to keep yours."

He slammed the door in her stunned face.

Chapter 9

As the lunch crowd at the soup kitchen dwindled, Dada wiped splatters around the food well. A week. It had started with Sion's abrupt dismissal of her and had gotten worse from there.

A new group of refugees had come through in the last few days, flooding the town with new mouths to feed, new stories to hear. But even with all the activity, it hadn't escaped her notice that Rosa hadn't shown with Carlos today.

Could Sion have sent her off sooner than the date on her ticket? Doubtful. Sion might not be speaking to her, but Rosa was. Dada had registered her in a hotel. She'd have known if the woman had checked out.

Alarm built in her chest. She turned to the sister beside her. "Have you seen Rosa today?"

Lifting a tray from the food well with a set of tongs, the sister looked around. "No." She shrugged. "That is typical behavior. She has continued her journey north."

"No, she hasn't. She wouldn't skip lunch. She has a small child to feed."

"Perhaps the child is sick."

Maybe. Dada put away the washcloth she'd been using. "I'm going to check where she's staying, just to make sure. Do you think anyone will mind?"

The sister dropped the tray with a clang. "*I* mind. You have been shirking your duties, and though Sister Angelica gives you leave to do so, I am not her. You will stay and do your job."

Praying for patience, recognizing the difficulty in putting together a new undercover identity, Dada picked up her pace.

#

After finishing her job, Dada went down the street to Rosa's hotel. Passing through archways lined with yellow painted pillars, she walked across the muted, multicolor tiles to the front desk. The manager recognized her and smiled. In no time at all, she was able to get him to give her an extra room key.

With the key in hand, Dada repeatedly knocked on Rosa's door. No answer.

Removing her small berretta Tomcat from a hidden pouch, she flicked off the safety and used the key to enter. The door beeped.

The room appeared clean, though the bed was unmade. There were no signs of a struggle. Slipping inside, she cleared the room, the bathroom, then went back for the closet.

Something rustled inside. Calm and focused, she slid the door open, then dropped to her knees before the sobbing little boy who had a shirt stuffed in his mouth to keep from making a sound.

She flicked on her weapon's safety, stowed it, and spoke to the boy in soothing tones. He calmed as she spoke. She put her arms out. After long coaxing moments, he rushed at her, threw his arms around her neck, and clung to her

Tears weren't weakness. Not his. Not hers. They were the cleansing before rebirth.

As Dada carried the shaking child out of the room, through the lobby, down the sidewalk and back toward the convent, she managed to get the boy to answer questions.

Kissing the child on his warm head, aware of the tears soaking her tunic, she prayed that Rosa was safe. Prayed she'd be returned. Prayed, although the only prayers she knew were the ones she'd learned for this mission.

The other sisters were returning from the soup kitchen when she neared the abbey. One rushed over. "Sister Dee? What has happened?"

"The mother," Dada explained. "She was taken, and I need to go back and speak with the police. Can you take the boy?"

The sister nodded.

"I need you to go with this kind woman," Dada gently explained to Carlos.

It took a few moments, but he agreed to go with the sisters.

One of them gently lifted him away and the other sisters gathered around the child, cooing to him, blessing him, soothing him with a loving kindness that was one of the dearest things she'd ever witnessed.

But now she had a mother to find.

#

Inside the traditionally decorated Mexican hotel lobby overrun with *policia* and a fussy hotel manager, Dada decided she thoroughly disliked Comandante

Javier Lopez. And not just because he wore sunglasses inside, but because he spoke down to her.

A half-foot shorter than her six feet, his tone still seemed to want to pat her on the head. "You see, my dear," Javier explained, "many women leave their children, so you are wasting your time. Go back and pray, Sister, and leave the investigations to us."

"Rosa didn't leave. She was taken."

"Her room was undisturbed," he said waving away another officer who approached. "You are jumping to conclusions."

Straightening her spine, willing herself not to seek the comfort of the bracelet on her wrist, she employed a tone as brisk as it was frustrated. "You are the one jumping to conclusions. This woman didn't abandon her child."

The Comandante shrugged. "My experience tells me otherwise, but you have a too-kind heart. I know the cold realities of this journey, of traveling to *El Norte*, because I've seen it before. You think she is the first woman to leave her child?"

Dada's fear and anxiety was morphing into stomach-turning rage. This man wasn't going to even try to find Rosa. Hadn't tried to find the women who'd gone missing in the past. Wouldn't try to find any that went missing in the future.

Of course, she knew the statistics. Due to the horrible drug wars, ninety-three percent of crimes in Mexico went unsolved. And those were just the reported crimes. Many crimes went unreported.

Logic told her not to push. Her "too-kind heart" said not pushing him didn't bring lost women home. "If you never search for them how can you know they have left their children? How can you know they weren't taken?"

His disturbed frown etched puppet lines around his round chin. "You live an entirely different life from these people, from us. You are sheltered. Taken care of. You don't know what you're talking about. The rules here aren't made by God, Sister. They're made by men."

Javier lifted his sunglasses and stared at her with brown foggy eyes. "Men like me."

For a moment, his statement stood between them, as solid and immovable as the bars on a prison. She could continue to challenge him, but to what end? It would only serve to draw her more surely under his scrutiny. An examination she could ill afford assuming, as she did now, that he knew more about these disappearances than he was saying.

Adopting the same confident calm Sister Angelica wore, she turned with a, "God sees all, Comandante."

"Then he must be blind."

Chapter 10

Seated at his workstation, eyes tired and sore from the long day, Sion examined every last detail, down to the minute edges of the photo on the passport. It was perfect.

His cell buzzed. Reaching into his pocket, he answered. "Oye."

"She's gone," Dee said.

How'd she get his number? Leaning back in his chair, he gripped the phone. "Who?"

"Rosa. I think she's been disappeared. Can you help me find her?"

A knot formed in his throat. He dropped Rosa's passport, got to his feet, and began to pace. "What did the police say?"

A sigh more fury than frustration rolled through the line. "I spoke with a Comandante Javier. He believes she abandoned her child. I believe he makes broad assumptions."

He paused on a floorboard that cracked under him. "I know of him. A few years ago, the fiancée of the bloke whose mum owns this building went missing."

"Do you mean Geraldo? He had a fiancée who went missing?"

His eyes traveled to his front door, remembering the first time Geraldo had brought him here. “Aye. That’s what he told me. Instead of trying to find her, the comandante blamed him, tried to pin Geraldo for her disappearance. Determined to clear his name and find her, Geraldo did his own investigation. No one knows exactly what happened, but he was found half-dead with his skull smashed in. He’s never been the same.”

“That’s awful. I spoke with him. I assumed…” She paused, and if it was possible to hear a woman thinking, he heard her. “I feel badly. I treated him as if he might not understand.”

“Most people do. It’s partly why he lost his phone service job and had to move back in with his mom and become the super. But he’s as sharp as a knife. A mechanical wizard and a good man.”

“Do you think he could have information for us? That maybe whoever took his fiancée could be the same person who has taken Rosa?”

Sion’s eyes sought out his most recent painting. Dee and Rosa walking across the *zocola*, with Carlos following behind. Bugger. Even if it was the same guy, it was doubtful Geraldo would remember. “I’ll ask him. But I don’t want to give you false hope, Sister—

“Dee.”

“Dee. He forgets much of what happened that night. Hate to trigger bad memories asking things he’ll have no recollection of.”

“I understand. But he is our only lead right now. He and the mysterious man who offered Rosa the job. And I’ve already begun asking around after him. I’m in the square now, speaking with refugees.”

"Alone at night? When a woman has gone missing?"

"I can take care of myself. Jiu jitsu, remember?"

He rubbed a hand around his tensing neck. "I'll go talk to Geraldo now. Let's meet after. I can help you interview people. They might respond better to Juan the Forger than Dee the Nun."

Another pause. Longer. "I should have thought of that. Perhaps I should change."

"Change into what?"

"Call me after. We can decide where to meet."

She hung up before he could respond.

Bugger.

#

Sion's bum leg decided tonight was the night it was going to remind him how pathetic it was. His usually light tread sounded clunky, like Captain Hook working his way across the bow of the *Sea Devil*. He hung onto the stair rail, trying to lessen the echoing sound.

Hitting the last step, he noticed someone in the shadows. Instinct took over. He shifted feet and raised his hands.

Geraldo came out from the dark corner. Sion let out a relieved breath. "Mate, I've told you to meet me here, not lurk."

Geraldo frowned, clomped his feet up and down.

True. Sion probably wouldn't have heard him anyway. "Fine. I'll give you a pass on the heart attack. Appreciate you meeting me out here. I know your mum is watching her *telenovela*. I didn't want to bother her."

Geraldo's blue eyes lit. His mouth twitched. "It's not wise."

"Exactly my thinking." *And* that he didn't want to upset Yolanda with talk of her son's missing fiancée. Yolanda had been there that night Geraldo had first spoken to Sion of his fiancée. She'd helped her son fill in a lot of the details but had cried repeatedly. It had been a heartbreaking evening. "I'm on my way out. Can you walk with me to my car?"

Surprise on his face, Geraldo put his hands into the pockets of his coveralls. "Yes."

Outside, they walked the darkening streets toward the lot where Sion had his car. Geraldo kept pace with Sion's troubled steps. Which meant, to Sion's mind anyway, that he was slowing down.

"Mate, I'm sorry to bring this up."

Geraldo's head swung his way.

Sion couldn't help another flash of guilt. He'd met Geraldo on the day he'd arrived in Oaxaca. Sion had been wandering about looking like a homeless person. Which, in fact, he had been. Geraldo had started talking to him. First in Spanish and then in English. Finding a room to rent and a friend had been that easy.

"I was talking to Sister Dee today."

Geraldo's brown skin turned russet. He jerked his head away as they crossed the street. "Doesn't look like a nun."

Sion laughed. "Glad I'm not the only one who thinks so, but trust me, don't say it out loud. Hugely offensive."

Geraldo's head swung back, eyes wide. "You didn't."

"Bach, she was so lush I couldn't help it. The words slipped past my lips before I could retrieve them."

Not the only thing to slip past his lips when it came to Dee.

Geraldo grinned and nodded. Felt good to be understood. And Geraldo did understand.

Although his hesitant way of talking and the fact that he sometimes skipped words led some to believe Geraldo wasn't all there, the truth was, he was sharp as a skinner's knife. Still, communication wasn't in his Strengths column.

That's why it was best to be direct with him. Cut down the back and forth. "A refugee woman has gone missing."

Geraldo hissed through his teeth, a sound a man recently punched in the gut might make. Sion's stomach tightened.

"Sorry, mate. I know this can't be easy on you, and I know you don't remember much about your own investigation into your fiancée…"

Geraldo's ham-fist came up to knock on his own head. "Not in there."

Poor guy. He'd spent months in the hospital recovering. "Anything you can remember? Even something before the"—*accident* wasn't the right word—"incident?"

Sion took out his keys as they approached his car. They stopped.

Squeezing his eyes closed, Geraldo's whole body seemed to tense. A single tear trailed down his cheek.

Sion put a palm against his shoulder and told him not to worry about it, but Geraldo's eyes popped open, immobilizing him.

With uncooperative fingers, Geraldo groped at the pocket on his coveralls. He took out his wallet and pulled out a piece of soiled folded notebook paper. He handed it to Sion.

Sion tried to decipher the faded numbers. "GPS coordinates?"

Geraldo pointed one dirt-encrusted finger at the paper. "Had it on me. Kept it." He tossed his head to the night sky and groaned in deep frustration. "Nothing there. Looked dozen times."

"So you had this on you when they found you with your head bashed in?"

He nodded.

"Is this where you were found?"

Geraldo shook his head.

Not where he'd been found, but he'd had it on him. Maybe he'd been checking a few spots? Or maybe it was nothing. "And you've checked this area at least a dozen times before?"

"Aye."

"Oh, *aye*, is it?" Sion grinned. "We'll make a Welshman of you yet."

"*Bugger*, not likely."

Sion full-out laughed. The man was clever. And if Geraldo, who knew the area, couldn't find anything, what were *his* chances? Still, he memorized the coordinates. He handed the paper back, then slapped him on the shoulder. "Thanks, mate. Take it easy."

As he turned to go, Geraldo grabbed him. The warmth in his blue eyes went cold. "Careful. Dangerous."

A flush of cold energy worked its way down his spine, setting the hair at his neck flying. "I promise to be careful."

Chapter 11

It was full dark when Sion pulled up to the corner where he and Dee had planned to meet. A long-legged woman in black jeans, black boots, black jacket, and knit hat stood on the corner, hot enough to make him do a double and triple take.

She walked forward. Oh. Good. Lord. It couldn't be. The richness of her skin, the sway of those hips, the length of those legs, long enough to wrap…

It was. Sister Dee.

Fine then, the Devil won this round.

Hell.

It would have to be Hell.

She knocked on the window. Swallowing his very inappropriate declaration and his tongue, he lowered it. She leaned in, bringing all that lush and the scent of rose water.

Honey-brown eyes twinkled with her smile. Those eyes. A man could get lost in them.

"A lime-green Cadillac, such a lovely car color."

He nodded, grinning like an idiot. The thing in his throat that was supposed to operate airflow, allowing him to utter words, blocked up completely.

She gestured at the car. "Are you going to unlock the car?"

Fuck. The door, mate. Mouth still seeking air, he hit the unlock button.

She went around to the other side, threw a backpack onto the floor, then slid into her seat with one long leg leading the way. He'd thought she was beautiful in her habit. That getup had dulled her. As had her contacts. "Those are your eyes."

Reaching up, she removed the hat from her head. "I'm surprised you could tell. Yes. The brown are my contacts."

It was the first time he'd seen her hair. Shorn tight against her scalp, *elegant* came to mind. His hand itched to run along the edges of her face, her perfect ear, her beautiful jaw.

Looking away, he put the car into drive. "The GPS coordinates are over an hour from here, Sister."

"Dee."

"For a nun, you sure don't like to be called Sister."

Her fingers moved to the leather bracelet on her wrist. "I'm an undercover nun. Thus, the outfit. Which, by the way, was a good suggestion."

Had she changed at his suggestion? Somehow, he felt she was a step ahead, not behind, him. He wished he could trust her. Damn, why did he feel like she'd manipulated him?

Everything in him told him she was not a nun—she didn't move like a nun, didn't act like a nun, sure as hell didn't kiss like a nun. And, yeah, mind-altering desire clouded his judgment, but logic also told him her being a nun made no sense.

He'd done research into the group she'd claimed to be from, and though it was possible, it was unlikely.

Still, he hadn't had the time to disprove it. So, for

now, he'd have to take her at her word. Which meant that she was a nun.

And he was a heathen.

With a, "Seatbelt, Sis—Dee," Sion headed onto the highway, toward the forty-acre property that his research told him the coordinates fell in the middle of.

#

It was nearly midnight when they reached as close to the coordinates as they were going to get. Sion pulled over to the side of the dirt road, parking over scrub and brush. His Cadillac had done okay on the dirt highway, but no way could it make it over the brush and large stones that blocked them from the exact coordinates.

Dada reached into the bag on her lap, and he flinched as she pulled out a gun. Hands tight on the wheel, it took him a moment to understand that she was explaining the weapon to him. "I'll not be carrying that."

"But—"

"No, luv. Put it away. I won't touch that thing."

Her eyes dropped to his leg. "Oh. I hadn't considered."

He gnashed his teeth together. "Don't consider it. Please. Don't."

She put the gun back into her bag and went silent. He waited for the questions or sympathy—*Does your leg hurt? I'm so sorry, how tragic*, or something else that tried to lay claim to his injury or dismiss it.

But she said, "Do you remember that game in the FAA Cup when you scored three goals and single-handedly defeated a team in the Premiere League?"

An uncontrollable smile rolled across his mouth. "Best game of my life."

Her eyes swung to him, pinned him. "I watched the whole thing online. Me, cross-legged on my bed, laptop in front of me, a pillow hugged to my chest, and..." She licked her lips. "It was so early in the morning, I kept burying my mouth into my pillow, biting it, screaming into it while I watched you. Oh, you were so beautiful.

"The way you slashed madly down the field, glided and spun and bulldozed. I was captured. When the game was over, I was shaking. Heart full and heartbroken all at once. I never thought to see the likes of that stunning performance again."

She paused, shook her head, then lowered her lashes. "But then, years later, you walked into a soup kitchen, and my heart leapt, and everything I had felt that day happened all over again. And my heart was full and broken all at the same time."

His throat closed up and his heart pounded. She saw him. *Him*. It made no difference to her if he was sprinting with all his pre-injury skills down the pitch or limping down the cafeteria line waiting to be served free food.

"When you asked why I don't see you as a nun, I had tidy answers. None true." He shouldn't do this. He shouldn't; it wasn't right. "But the truth was—is—I can't see you as a nun because that's a role, an identity that slips from my eyes every time I look at you. I see fire and grace, a woman—black and beautiful, sexy and determined, gentle and fiery. And it doesn't matter what costume you put on, what's on your head, hands, or your feet, I will always see that woman when I look at you."

An unspoken, boiling need lit her eyes, lit his body. They leaned across the seat toward each other.

Heaven be damned. Give Satan his due.

Their lips met in a wild joining that exploded in an instant and intense, throwing-caution-to-the-wind fire.

The heavy tangle of their breaths, the magnetic pull of their bodies, had him reaching under her shirt, delighting in her tender and full breast. Had her fumbling for the button on his jeans, running a hand over his aching hardness, moaning into his mouth.

A howl from a coyote, close enough to raise the hair on his arms, arrested their movement. They threw themselves back at nearly the same instant, with nearly the same brutal force, bumping into their seats.

Breath heavy, as loud as his heartbeat, he adjusted himself. And for that one moment all that existed between them was unapologetic heat.

When their breathing was more even, she said, "Are you ready?"

His affection for her ratcheted up another notch. Or seven. "Born ready."

Chapter 12

Armand dragged the girl down the basement stairs. The *puta* fought like a panther. She swung, missed, tried again, and scratched his arm.

"Let me go!" she screamed. "My son needs me!"

"He does not need a whore,' Armand said, kicking her legs out from under her.

She fell against him, unbalancing him as he dragged her across the room.

Her gaze took in the room with the metal chains embedded in the walls, the bloody mattresses, the knives, the drill. "What is this place?"

"It's a funhouse, *puta*," he said, grabbing her by the hair and raising her to face him. "If you didn't look just like her, I'd show you how much fun it can be."

"No. No," she said, still wrestling against him, dragging her feet against the bloody cement floor. "You took me, because I look like another? That is why?"

"The accident of your birth," Armand said, kicking her again. "Like mine, like all of us. It defines the destiny of every person on this planet. Though some would tell you otherwise. They lie."

"Let me go. Please. My son. He is alone."

"That is your fault. I sent men with money, but you let a whore buy you a room."

"Do you mean Sister Dee?" She jerked away, swung. "She is no whore!"

He hit her in her face. She put up her hands to protect herself. He punched again. "Your room was paid for by a whore and with whore's money."

His knuckles slammed against her hands, the strikes and her muffled cries sending desire surging through him. It wasn't until blood dripped through her fingers, until her broken hands dropped from her face that he stopped.

He let go. She fell onto the slab floor and laid still. He spit on her, handcuffed her to a water pipe. This was all Dada's fault.

Merde. What a mess.

He checked her pulse. Still alive.

He wiped the blood on his pants. Hands shaking, he pulled out his phone and texted Walid to let him know his "merchandise" had been found and that it would be shipped to the buyer in a couple days.

The text came back. "Two days."

Armand sighed and stared at the blood-stained woman. Things had been so much easier before Dada came. She was a curse. One that he desperately needed to get rid of. His hands ached with the need for a revenge that had been decades in the making.

He texted his partner. "Do you still have eyes on her? Is she still asking after the girl?"

A few moments later the response came. "She left the city with the forger."

The forger? Fury rolled up from his stomach as thick and heavy as acid. He spat it out with a curse, texted with rage filling his skull. His thumbs pounded each key. It was time to end this.

He hit SEND.

Chapter 13

Dada gathered her backpack and NVGs, then stepped from the car and surveyed the area. What she could see of it. It was flat. Stars brighter than any she'd ever seen and a glorious, partial moon.

Sion got out of the car and hit a button. The trunk popped up with a click. She walked around to it.

A shovel, rope, highway flares, and toolbox lined the trunk's dingy black fabric. Grabbing the shovel and propping it against the taillight, she placed her backpack in the trunk, unzipped the clamshell and shoved rope and road flares inside.

Sion removed a headlamp from the toolbox and turned it on. Not really necessary in the moonlight, but he'd disabled all the car lights, even the trunk.

He picked up the shovel, laid it across one shoulder, then they headed across the desert.

He pointed at her goggles. "What are those?"

"Night vision goggles, but I doubt we'll need them."

He put his headlamp on his head and nodded. "This'll do."

Two hours later, they came to the coordinates, so said the app developed by her sister Gracie. It was not available to the public. That was one of the best things about being a League operative—access to things that no one else could get their hands on.

"Let's split up to search," she said.

"Good idea."

He got to work. Never once did he complain about his leg, but she'd noticed his gait had gotten worse as they'd walked.

"*Ach-y-fi.*" Sion tripped over a bit of brush with a hop-skip. He bent down to rub his leg. "Things got daggers."

"You okay?"

"Fine. Watch the bushes."

She smiled as he gave the shrubs a wide berth. Hmm, *watch the bushes*. That reminded her of a mission in Costa Rica where the entrance to an underground hideout had been beneath a flowering plant.

Putting on protective gloves, she went to the nearest shrub and pulled. Nothing. And to the next… Again, nothing.

"What are you doing?"

"Once on a mission—" She cursed internally as she grasped the top of a dead bush, fully expecting its withered roots to silently give way, but there was a creak of steel and wood.

"What the hell?" Sion said.

Holding up a finger, heart pounding, she pulled the shrub the rest of the way open. She bent to the hole and scanned the outside. The brush was attached to a rusted lid and circular ring that reminded her of a submarine. The mechanics were rudimentary. No alarms. Hugging the inside of the dirt walls, welded to the metal ring around the opening, was a ladder.

Sion knelt beside her. “Let me go.”

She put a finger to her lips and shook her head. The creak was loud enough to alert someone to their presence, but no need to give information that might help anyone who might be hiding down there. Like the number of people up here.

Dropping her backpack, she removed a thin steel, bendable cord. When she inserted it into her cell, the end of the tube lit up.

Kneeling by the side of the lid, she pulled the cord longer, lowered the end into the chamber. An image appeared on her phone screen. A 360-sweep revealed a five-by-five space tightly packed with boxes and a shelving unit with pottery jars at the back.

Hmm. Storage? She zoomed closer to the jars. There was a door behind the jars.

Sitting down, she dropped her legs over the mouth of the opening.

Sion grabbed her arm.

She looked up at him, at the concern on his face. “It’s empty,” she mouthed.

With a nod, he let go of her.

Heart rocking harder than a drum solo, she took out her gun, flicked down her goggles, then dropped over the side.

As her feet hit the compact earth in the underground storage facility, she realized she would’ve been better off with thermal goggles. NVGs required more ambient light. Still, she could see fairly well. Gun raised; she scanned the darkness.

She neared the shelving unit, peered around the jars, and inspected the rusted steel door. The handle and lock looked new. This place was still in use.

Chances were good that this area extended beyond what was visible.

Lords and ladies, the League needed to add more underground warfare to their roster. A firefight in an underground lair would prove a challenge.

One arm on the top rung, Sion lowered himself down. The area was a comfortable height for her, but he had to bend his six-foot-seven frame at the neck. He scanned the area with his headlamp.

Keeping her eyes down to avoid any glare through her glasses, she twitched her chin in the direction of the shelving unit. His light fell on it. He signaled to let her know he'd seen it.

As soundlessly as possible, she visually inspected the jars. No trip wires. She looked under the shelves. No sensors. She slid a few jars. They weren't attached to anything. She scanned the legs of the shelving unit. Nothing.

They could move it without fear of setting off an alarm.

A glance over her shoulder showed her that Sion was making the same inspection of the rest of the chamber. He was a quick study.

She helped him clear the rest of the area, and then they moved back to the rack. With a few sweeps of her hands, she told him what she needed him to do. He nodded. They moved the jars first, placing them in a corner. And then, together, they lifted and slid the metal rack far enough back to allow the door to open.

Once cleared, the door, rusted and ancient, practically dared them to enter. Her hands sweated in her gloves. Scanning the door closely, she couldn't find any alarms. Obviously, no one had expected company in a place in the middle of the desert, miles from humans, hidden under a shrub. No wonder Geraldo had never found it.

Dropping her backpack, she unzipped a side pocket and took out her lock-picking kit. It took her a few moments to pick open the new locks.

With a signal to Sion, she kept her gun raised, providing him cover. He grabbed the handle and heaved open the rusted door with one brutal yank. A burst of dust and underground air choked with a rotting, rancid smell pushed out.

She gagged, turned her head. Sion put his arm up and buried his nose in the crook of his elbow. He issued a low, pained keen that let her know he was familiar with the smell of death.

Behind the door lay a tunnel braced by wood beams. It sloped downward, preventing her from seeing far inside. Dropping her bag again, she pulled out a compact tactical medical kit. She removed two paper masks, the kind a doctor might wear. Better than nothing.

After they put them on, she signaled him, advancing past him down the unknown hollow.

He followed.

The tunnel expanded and broke off into earthen side chambers stacked with varying levels of decomposing corpses.

"Fuck." Sion threw his light along the bodies. He began to scan. "Not here. Not here. Oh, Sophia, please don't be in here. Not here."

His gloved hand reached out to one and then another body. He pushed hair from a face. A heartbreaking choked sound muffled by his mask.

"Is it her? Sophia?"

"Too old," he said, placing his hand over her eyes. He lowered his head. "Who would do this?" he whispered.

Dada put a hand on his arm. "Sion."

He dropped his arm and turned to her. "I… So many." He wiped his eyes with the back of his hand. "Whatever information you need, whatever I can help with, anything. I'll do anything to bring these fuckers to justice."

Finding herself struck wordless with affection for him, wordless in the middle of this nightmare, she nodded, silently promising these women that the person responsible for this would pay. Even if that person wasn't part of the mission she was technically here for.

Swallowing her distress, she asked, "Do you have a photo of Sophia? This will go quicker if we are both looking for her and Rosa."

And she needed it to go quickly. Even if Sion's heavy breaths and anguished eyes didn't tell her he would soon lose it, the toxic stew of decaying bodies would have prompted her unease. They gave off hydrogen sulfide, carbon dioxide, and methane.

He reached into his pocket. He took out a photo of a young girl. A child sitting at an easel, painting.

She glanced up at him. "Who is she?"

He swallowed. "After football, I had a long recovery. It changed me and made me want to help others. So I went and taught art therapy in El Salvador. That's where I met Sophia." He let out a long breath. Anger this time. Better anger than sadness. "After they killed her father, they came into my class. It was five against one. Hard as I fought, they took Sophia from my class." He shook his head. "I had to convince her father, had to convince so many parents, to let the kids come to class. It's my fault."

Dada's heart trembled, cracked, and fell to pieces in her chest. This was it. Why he was here. She'd wondered, but nothing had made sense. "You changed your life, aligned with organized crime, worked for Walid to find this girl? That's why you're here?"

A long moment of silence and then a broken, "Let's look for them."

She didn't need him to explain all the details; she understood. "If Sophia's not here, and I pray she isn't, I will help you find her. Promise."

With a nod that seemed all he could manage, Sion tucked away the photo. The stench of death soaked into their clothes. The quiet of the underground tomb surrounded them. Neither spoke as they bent to the gruesome task, holding hope that two lives had been spared this awful fate.

Chapter 14

Sweat and salt drenched Sion's brow. Hard to remember ever feeling this beat down.

Thirty-one women. No Sophia or Rosa. Some bodies were simply too decayed to be them. The women who were here had been shot, tortured, brutalized. The signs were obvious even to someone like him, who'd never seen the like.

He dropped his light from the face of another woman who'd never had a chance. "We're going to need to alert the police."

Dee rolled her neck and stood from where she'd been squatting. "Agreed."

A noise like thunder erupted. Dee spun, moved like fire, sprinting at him. "Down!"

A spasm of heat and pressure, dirt and grit slammed down the tunnel and lifted Dee. A millisecond later it hit Sion, tossing him to the ground. Something dropped across his back, knocking the air from his lungs. Face pressed into dirt, fighting for air, he shifted as creaks and groans settled around him.

Ears ringing, crap leg barking pain, he rolled dirt and debris from his back as he sat up. Air coated with dust rushed into his lungs. *Fuck*, lost his mask. He bent forward, gagged into his fist. Spit repeatedly.

With a tug of his shirt over his nose and mouth, he breathed again, trying to make out something—anything—in the dark. Couldn't see. He'd lost his headlamp. "Dee? Dee, are you hurt?"

"I'm fine," came the reply amid a series of hacking coughs. A light flicked to his left. "You?"

What good would it do to tell her his leg felt like someone had taken a hatchet to it? None. "Aye. What happened?"

"An explosive booby trap." She sounded groggy. "Not sure how I missed it or why it took so long to go off, but it did."

Her light dropped from him and flashed down the tunnel, sparkling off floating particles of dust. "Let's get out of here."

Rolling to a crouch, he inched his way forward. Dee helped, shining her light across the area that separated them. The sight was more gruesome than ever, with sightless eyes and broken limbs.

"The dirt covering them should help with the escaping toxins," she said, almost to herself, but he'd noticed she, too, no longer had her mask.

"Hold your light there," he said, spotting his headlamp. He picked it up, cuffed off the dirt, tested it. Still worked. "I've got it."

She lowered the light from him and flashed it down the tunnel. When he was next to her, she pointed the light back down at his leg. "You're hurt."

"One to talk," he said. "Your forehead is bleeding."

She put a hand up to her bleeding head. "And my backpack is buried, along with our water, and other supplies. I'm usually much luckier than this."

"Well, if it's any consolation, you're the luckiest woman down here."

She snorted. Without another word they moved down the tunnel.

Sion was already bent double when the roof and sides forced him to get to his knees and crawl. Despite nerve-rattling shifts, pops, and squeals, along with their coughing and gagging, the area had a muffled quality.

"Good thing we weren't in the front chamber," he said as he was forced to worm-crawl. The beams in the back had held, saving them. His hands bit into stones and bones. He put it from his head as he followed her through a narrowing passageway. Eventually, and much to his surprise, the passage widened a bit—enough that he could crawl up beside her and stare at the sloped wall of dirt that blocked the exit.

He flashed his light along it. Debris. Jars. Glass. Beams.

"Look here," Dee said, directing her light into the slope of dirt.

He looked. There was a hole the size of toddler's head.

"Can you move over a touch, so I can get closer?"

She squeezed to her side, allowing him to shimmy closer and examine it. It was a hole. Went deep, too. The explosion had collapsed the tunnel, but beams had fallen in a way that left a small opening. He looked at her. "You *are* lucky."

"The luckiest woman down here."

He grunted, then stuck his hand in the hole. Unbelievable. He could put his whole arm up and not reach the end of it. Thought he could feel air. Not possible. Still… "I can dig us out of here, but it might take a while."

"We have until the chemicals from the decaying bodies kill us or we run out of air. Perhaps three hours."

No pressure. "Right, then. Let's find a shovel, so I can get started."

"We need a buttress," she said. "Digging out could cause a collapse."

"Not today. In this, too, you're lucky."

"Why is that?"

"When I was a child, my da, disreputable banker that he was, had me dig hidey-holes each time we moved."

"I take it you moved a lot."

"Let's just say, if there's one thing I know how to do, it's dig a hole."

Chapter 15

Dada did not give up easily. She also did not ignore reality. They were running out of air. Sickness and exhaustion had set in. Of course, her luck would win out. It always did, right?

Face covered in sweat, nausea rocking her stomach, her neck ached and her hot breath soaked the dirt in the tightly packed area they'd dug out—about the width and length of a coffin. She scratched again at the material above her. Steel. A portion of the door to the upper chamber.

She tried to press on it, lift it, but it wouldn't budge. No telling how much dirt lay beyond it, so they needed to find a way around this metal blockade.

Whichever direction they chose to dig could be the most important decision of their lives, because if they choose wrong… if that choice led them to more doors, more debris, and not to a place that could be easily dug around, they were dead.

Panting, sliding the shovel down as she shimmied backward, she exited into the wider chamber beside Sion.

They'd decided one person should dig while the other stayed still, using less air. She handed him the headlamp.

He took it. "My turn?"

She nodded, dizzy. The air was thick, their breathing heavy, which poisoned the air every time they exhaled.

She pulled the flashlight from her pocket and pointed it through the area they'd dug out. They might die down here. Oh, she was usually better at holding back tears. "But my luck never… fails. Never."

Sion grabbed her arm. "Luv, don't cry."

She covered her face with her hands, trying to hide her desperate tears. "So tired. Can't. Catch. My breath."

"*Luv.*" He pulled her hand away, kissed her cheek and the tears that trailed down her face. She welcomed the warmth of his touch. It might be the last and only comfort they had to give each other.

Sion moved his mouth to her ear. "Would've liked a lifetime to get… to know… you."

Gooseflesh tingled and cascaded down her body. There was nothing left but that immediate truth between them. The reality of this situation required honesty. Escape was near impossible. There was too much debris and chances were slim they'd find a way past that door.

She kissed his sweat-and-dirt-stained lips. "I'm not a nun."

He laughed, gently against her lips. "No shit."

Their lips collided and greedily used up oxygen. Heart aching in her chest, she contented herself with this, as all the passion of a not-likely lifetime broke free from where it lay hidden. So short of breath, darkness tinged her consciousness, but she still didn't break the kiss.

He, however, did.

He gripped her face in his hands and wiped her tears with his thumbs. “My turn.”

His hope touched her. Rallied her. “Yes. A. Lifetime. Awaits.”

Sion shimmied back into the dug-out area. She slid the shovel to him.

The sound of his digging quickly followed. She reached for her leather bracelet, thought of her son, closed her eyes and drifted off…

She jostled awake as he slid back into their shared grave. He gripped her arm, brought his forehead to hers. “Broke through.”

He held out the headlamp. She reached and missed, then concentrated on the light, reaching again with arms that felt encased in three winter jackets, and grabbed it. “Yes!”

He grunted, closed his eyes.

Unable to even wipe the sweat from her eyes or put the headlamp on, she willed all her energy into going back into that stifling tube of dirt. So tired. She wiggled upward, shoulders and elbows, rocking forward.

Panting, she reached the end. Ah, Sion had chosen to dig above the door. Good choice. Or so it had turned out. The area he’d dug was wide enough for her head. And there was air.

She breathed it in. Weeping, she reached through the hole and her hand slapped against a metal bar. It halved the opening. *Oh no*.

They had minutes of air left below. Only one person could be in this space breathing freely.

Sobs. She couldn’t stop the sobs. He would not

survive down there. And he expected her to take advantage of the work he'd done, breathe this air, free herself.

No.

Squeezed into the tight opening, she used numb fingers to feel the beam and the area Sion had started to dig around. Sion passed her the shovel, sliding it by her thigh.

She grasped it. Fuck this. Let the whole thing crash down, crush her. Or let this damn bar break and give them both freedom.

Using the tip and giving a big what-do-I-have-to-lose, she slammed the shovel into the metal. One. Two times.

"Whoa. It could collapse. Stop!"

She ignored him. The metal bent. She hit it again. A rumbling. She stopped. The ground shifted. Dirt poured down and across her face.

Shaking her head and blinking, she looked back up. She had a moment of confusion, but then her mind put words to images.

A snuffling muzzle, sharp teeth, scratching paws. An animal. It dug at a wild pace, expanding the opening, inching toward her. Dirt continued to sift down across her. Coyote or wolf, she couldn't tell, but its paws moved with fury.

Dada scurried back to Sion. "Coyote. Coming."

"Digging down?"

"Yep."

He panted. "Good. God."

She nodded. They shimmied backward down the tunnel. She held the shovel as a weapon, ready to fight as best she could in the tight space.

"If it makes it…." He trailed off.

"Yes," she said, understanding. This animal could dig past the beam, free them. Then, of course, they'd be stuck in a tight space with a wild animal.

Long minutes later, they heard the animal burrowing down through the tunnel. Hoping to scare it, Dada let out a, "Get out!"

Sion pounded on the ground. Actions that cost their beleaguered bodies.

The animal kept coming. If anything, it came faster.

Lying on her stomach, Dada hooted and whistled and held the shovel blade pointed toward the opening. Sion had inched ahead of her and grabbed a sharp, broken bit of wood.

The truth was, the space was too tight. They were in no condition to battle a wild animal. And if there was more than one?

Whining, snuffling noises echoed down the tunnel. The air seemed to grow less dense.

Dada's shoulders dropped and she focused on the round hole amid the slope of caved-in dirt, her senses ready.

The animal broke through in a mad rush of galloping limbs and heavy panting. Dada cried out as it charged past Sion toward her.

Madness. She dropped the shovel, and used her hands to fend off the attack. The dog barked, licked, sniffed her, moving around her in an excited bout of joy. Leaving her, perhaps not getting the frantic appreciation it wanted, it ran over to Sion.

Sion petted the groping, wet muzzle, whispered, "Good lad."

A dog. A dog was here. Darting between them. Begging for love.

"It has a tag on its collar," Sion said.

Sion shone his flashlight at it. The dog closed its eyes, looked away, kept licking at them blindly. At least he was friendly. "There's no name, but there's a phone number and an address in Texas."

"Texas!" Dada slapped a hand to her mouth. The owner of the property maybe? Or whoever had buried the bodies. Perhaps they were more sophisticated than Dada had thought and had a device here that let them know the explosion had happened so they'd sent a dog down?

Sion shimmied forward. "Might be dangerous up there. Let me go."

A shake of her head that reminded her how exhausted she was. "No, I will. I'm experienced. I'm…"

"Woman, give me this. Let me follow Tex out."

"Tex?"

"Short for Texas."

"You named this dog?

Chapter 16

His bum leg leaning against the dew-covered edge of his car, the headlights of a pickup truck illuminating him, Sion once again shook the hand of Manuel Arturo Peña, the man who owned the chocolate lab who'd rescued them.

"Are you sure I can't offer you a reward, Manuel? You and Tex, uh Gambit, saved our lives."

Kneeling by the car, petting Gambit, Dee added, "We'd much prefer to give you something."

Manuel, a Mexican man with a Texas twang and matching cowboy hat, said, "No, sir. You guys were lost in the desert and had a hell of a night. 'Sides, Gambit did his job and rescued you both. That's what he's meant to do."

Though they'd told Manuel they'd been lost and trapped, they hadn't filled him in on the gory details. During the walk back, Manuel—who'd been combing acres in his pickup looking for Gambit—had pulled up. He'd given them some water and a ride to their car, and also bandaged Dada's head.

Manuel tipped back his hat. "Don't want to alarm you or put you off on hiking, but you should stick to known trails next time. Rumor says this area is owned by a trafficker."

Dee stood. "Do you mean Walid Grimale?"

His eyebrows rose. "I was never given any one name."

There was a beat of silence in which Sion felt that Manuel very much reevaluated them.

Dee, perhaps feeling it too, bent again to Gambit, who licked her face. "He's going to make a great search-and-rescue dog."

"That's the hope, ma'am," he said, turning toward his truck. "If y'all are okay, we're going to get going."

"We are. Thanks," Sion said, kneeling with a groan to thank Gambit one last time. The chocolate lab licked his face like they were old friends.

Manuel whistled, holding the door open for Gambit, who darted away and into the cab of the pickup.

The trucked backed up, turned around, and drove off. With the headlights no longer shining on them, the area seemed foreboding. Dee was already slipping into the car, so he joined her.

Sion glanced at Dee. "I'd thought your luck was a made-up thing, but it's been verified by circumstance."

"Being rescued by a runaway dog is irrefutable proof?"

He reversed, turned the vehicle around, then headed down the moonlit desert road. "A runaway dog being trained for search-and-rescue. Yes. Definitely."

All the pieces that had to come together floored Sion. Manuel lived in Texas but was having difficulty training Gambit. He'd brought him here for extra training from his cousin, an expert, who lived in a village outside of Oaxaca.

If the dog hadn't been having these issues, Manuel wouldn't have brought him to Mexico. Moreover, if he'd been fully trained, Gambit wouldn't have run after a cottontail and away from his owner, and he wouldn't have dug his way down to them. That was a bit of hot luck Sion could barely contemplate.

As they bumped down a dirt road back to Oaxaca, Dee glanced his way. "Perhaps, one day, I can tell you a truly remarkable story about my luck."

"Truly remarkable? Hard to imagine a story that outdoes this one. Go on, then."

The invitation to tell him that story fell flat and the silence of the car along the unpaved road seemed deafening.

A sudden tense awareness descended over them. Until this point, they had been riding the high of rescue, enjoying their luck, playing with Gambit, and telling Manuel a cleaned-up version of events.

Now, all that had happened underground—the tears, the scorching hot kiss, the truth that she wasn't a nun and he wasn't a forger, the vulnerability of the near-death experience—left something heavy, expectant between them.

"Maybe when you do tell me that story, you'll also give away who you work for."

She swiveled her head toward him, tilted it.

For a moment, all he could feel was her eyes taking him in. His body grew warm. Alert.

"Undoubtedly. Since they are tied together. But for now, trust my motivations are good."

He glanced at her. Dirt soiled her shirt, pants, and was smeared across her face. She was so lovely.

And not a nun.

Warmth suffused his body. His heart accelerated. He cared. More than cared. He needed her to trust him.

He turned onto a paved, empty highway. "Trust me. You can tell me who you work for. Whatever you're doing, I've got your back. I promise, Dee. I promise."

She grasped her leather bracelet. A habit he now realized was tied to stress.

"Even if my name isn't Dee?"

Bugger. That hurt. Then again, she only knew his by coincidence. "Even then."

A troubled frown spoiled her forehead. "Even if what I do isn't legal?"

Was she kidding? "It doesn't fucking matter. We didn't meet on the beach in Cancun. Or at a local gym. Or through an online dating app. We're here in the middle of something awful. The rules are different."

The luck lifesaving. The risks deadly. The feelings accelerated.

Hands flexing on the wheel when she didn't respond, he swung over to the side of the deserted road. He turned the car off, twisted in his seat to look at her. "Even if you never tell me your real name or who you're working for, as long as I know what you're going to do will stop horrors like what we saw tonight, I'm in."

She gaped at him. Such a look, so open and raw and filled with want that his body flushed with desire. He watched as she licked her lips, stared at his.

"Is your seat all the way back?"

"Aye."

Swinging her leg across, she straddled him, reached down, and yanked the recline lever. His head bumped against the leather.

Staring up at all that beauty, wanting her as much as he had ever wanted any woman, as hard as he'd been in his entire life, he was completely thunderstruck.

She was too lovely. His body thrummed. The temperature in the car seemed to have gone risen to a thousand. But he could not move.

She leaned down, kissed him lightly on the lips, writhed against his hard-on.

Blazing flames licked him, erupted through him, so thick and hot that he forgot everything that had ever been, every word said, every lie whispered for the very real, very deep and throbbing desire happening right now.

She began to grind against his aching cock. He gripped each of her round arse cheeks, helping himself to her.

Her kiss deepened and he welcomed her with everything he had. Their ragged breaths filled the rocking car. Her tongue glided, played joyfully against his. Stroking him, firing his breathing, his mind.

And despite his cynical nature, he felt there might be such a thing as destiny. Felt she spoke to him, felt she told him something with that kiss.

Chapter 17

Sion's kiss made Dada's head spin. His hand slipped from her butt and under her shirt. Dada broke it off, moved back to her seat.

"Sorry. Too fast?"

Not too fast. It was just, in this, *she* needed to be in charge.

She slipped her pants down her long legs and kicked them off. "I need for you to let me do everything, Sion. Okay?"

She took off her underwear.

"Yes. Okay. Yes."

As she pulled her shirt over her head, then stripped off her bra, Dada looked over at him.

Sion sat there, unmoving.

"Are you okay?"

"Not sure what's going on here?" Sion admitted. "And I really don't want to make assumptions."

She tried to hold back her delighted smile when she told him, "I want to have sex with you. Here, in this car. If you'd like to have sex with me, I will need you to take off your pants."

He whipped off his shirt, pulled down his pants and boxers so quickly that when he plopped his naked butt back in the seat, the car rocked, and his cock stood at attention, hard and ready and dripping.

Stupendous. She'd scared him stiff. Glancing down at his erection, she realized that wasn't a bad thing. Oh. That was so beautiful. She reached over and gripped him. "Is this okay?"

He closed his eyes. "More than okay."

"Do you have a condom?"

His eyes popped open. A panicked look and then relief, "Yes. Thank the Almighty. Glove compartment."

A gentle laugh, a soft breath released, she reached forward and found it. A rip of the wrapper, and she stroked the condom down to the base of him.

Straddling him again, she gripped his length, hard and throbbing in her hand, and lowered herself onto him with a moan. So good.

He let out a curse, thrust, pushing his cock deeper.

Oh. She rose, drove down again. Her moans filled the car, accelerating with her breaths.

Her thighs tightened around him, and her mouth joined to his. Her lips played against his as her tongue dove again and again into his mouth. The friction built. She increased her rhythm.

Unable to match her pace, he raised his hips with, "Yes. Luv. Fuck."

She took what she wanted and rode him with a wild abandon.

He gasped in her ear. "Slow. Going to lose it."

But she was so close. And he felt so good, so hard, and smooth. He filled every part of her as the delicious friction tightened her core. "Can't stop. Please, don't ask me to."

He grunted, kissed her sweetly along her neck. "I'll keep it up all day, then."

An exaggeration, she knew, but a hot enough promise that, as the coil of energy increased and the pressure rose to unbearable levels, she tossed her head back and lost herself with a cry of, "I'm coming. Oh, Sion, come with me."

His wet lips moaned against the slick skin of her neck. His strong hands squeezed her butt. A moment later, with her warm body frantically riding him, he came with a curse and a rush of warmth she could feel even through the condom.

Her pace slowed and she collapsed across him, sated. Exhausted. They fought to catch their breaths.

His hands released her cheeks, rubbed tenderly against her bottom. He whispered, "You've undone me, luv. You've completely undone me."

She relaxed in a half-awake, half-dream way. Slowly, she returned to the car and the coolness of the desert air through Sion's partially open window. The press of his sweat-soaked skin against hers. "Thanks for listening and letting me set the pace. I needed to connect, to make some memories other than the worst of this night."

He brushed a tear from her face that she hadn't known was there. He rubbed his nose across her cheek. "Ah, well, it was entirely to my benefit, but I'm not just a good listener when I'm being shagged by the hottest woman I've ever met. Care to give me a try? You could start with your real name."

Could she? Could she unmask herself before him? She wanted to, but she was also afraid. Her disguises kept her safe. Maybe. But to expose herself that fully required clothing. She wriggled from his lap back into the passenger seat.

She reached down and began to turn her clothes inside out. He watched her for a moment, and she felt a heavy pressure in his gaze, a longing. She understood. Already, she felt a loss without the closeness of him.

Sion's phone buzzed in the cup holder. They must be back within range. He looked at the screen. "Bugger."

"What's wrong?"

"Got a text from the head of security for the trafficker I do papers for." He showed her the text.

Meet me. Tomorrow night. I want to talk to you about the company you've been keeping.

Latching her bra, she leaned toward him. "There's a chance my cover is blown. I no longer have the element of surprise. I was warned not to involve myself looking for Rosa. Now, I'm on my own. I can't go to my people with this."

"I thought Rosa was your mission."

She slipped on her underwear. "Technically, my mission is to get information on Walid. Routes. Security. More and more, it seems finding Rosa is something separate."

"Security. Routes. That's information I can give you." Sion pulled up his boxers. "Walid's man, Armand Stoker, is easy to play. Huge temper. Bigger ego. Because of him, I've learned of three trafficking routes from El Salvador. I just need to pin down the one Sophia was taken on."

She shuddered. "That name."

"You know him?"

"I once knew two men, each had half of that name. A man whose first name was Armand. And another man whose last name was Stoker, Miles Stoker. The first man is currently a…" she swallowed, "scientist in French Guiana. The second man… I have no idea."

Jeans in hand, he stopped. "Armand has a French accent."

Cold brushed feathers down her skin. Could it be him? Walid did have routes through South America. And there was little Stoker knew better than keeping women hostage. Well, one thing… torturing women. She frowned. "It makes horrifying sense."

"It does?"

"Yes. Manuel said the land was owned by a trafficker. Walid is the only one in the area. But from the research I've done into his operation, he would never waste—" she grimaced, swallowed her distaste "—what he calls *product*. And what we saw tonight was a waste."

"So it could be someone with ties to Walid who knows about the property and enough about Walid's business to use the property without Walid's knowledge."

"Someone who was always a sadistic bastard." She pressed the bracelet at her wrist hard against her skin. "I shouldn't involve you further. This is not without risk. What I do. What I am going to do here."

"I've been looking for Sophia for a long time, and I know the danger, so if you're trying to warn me off, stop."

"Are you—"

"Yes."

She smiled at him. "You might be the luckiest thing that has ever happened to me."

"You'll let me help?"

"That depends."

"On what?"

"Does Armand ever search you for listening devices when you meet?"

Chapter 18

The convent sat quiet and dark in the early morning before prayers. Dressed like a thief, with her head bandaged, and smelling like sex and death, Dada slipped inside, closed the door silently behind her.

"Sister Dee."

Ah! Dada spun, grabbing hold of Sister Angelica as a matter of reflex. "I'm sorry, Sister. I'm not used to being snuck up on."

"I didn't sneak." She briskly brushed down her tunic. "I was standing here when you came inside, but you didn't see me."

Well, that didn't usually happen. A long night was no excuse. She'd gotten sloppy.

"Sister, I am very sorry to be breaking the rules like this. I can assure you—"

Sister Angelica turned on her heel. "Follow me."

Stupendous. Looked like Sister Angelica had reached the limit on her patience. Seemed her line was with her nuns sneaking out at night, disappearing during the day, avoiding chores, prayers, and church.

Dada followed Sister Angelica into a large office, well-stocked with books and a gorgeous cherry red Ukrainian desk. Four small statues were gathered on one corner, huddled together. Each one was a woman at a different age. From child to teen to young woman to nun.

Sister Angelica stood by her desk. "I can't have this, Sister Dee."

Dada felt her stubborn rise. She had a mission. Women were disappearing. Dying. "Sister Angelica, I am undercover. Surely you want me to find Rosa. Surely, you knew when Momma asked you to allow me to come here, that I'd be doing things that weren't very nun-like."

The older woman shook her head and met Dada's eyes with something that looked very much like disappointment. "Don't assume. It's an annoying American trait."

Dada huffed. She hadn't been born in America. But rather than follow Sister's assumption with impatience, she waited.

And waited. Sister Angelica's rapidly tap, tap, tapping foot against the tiles seemed to drag on and on. Dada's gaze slipped over the words of St. Catherine of Sienna's stenciled on the wall, *In the end, nothing that ever caused one pain will exist. No one will begrudge me.*

She hoped that was true. Hoped that all the pain of this world, all her pain, would one day be erased.

Finally, the older woman pushed her black-rimmed glasses up her nose. "I'd been going to say that I can't have you running around—"

"Sister—"

Sister Angelica snapped her cane against the tile floor. Dada had heard less concussive gunshots. "I can't have you running around trying to solve a puzzle when I have part of the answer."

The nun let that seep its way through the pores of Dada's overstressed brain before continuing. "Yesterday, when you told me you would search for Rosa, I should have said something, but I didn't want to break a confidence. I now believe it is the right thing to do."

"You know something about the disappearances?" Dada asked.

The woman leaned against her desk and angled her cane to the side. "Yes. There was a man who was accused of making his fiancée disappear. Geraldo Gonzalez."

Ugh. She already knew this. Hope disappeared into disappointment.

Sister Angelica watched her, a look on her face that was as old as it was wise. "The man who calls himself Geraldo Gonzalez isn't who he says he is."

"I'm not sure I understand," Dee said. "He's been here for decades, knows many in town. They know him. His fiancée."

"All true. What is not true is that his name is Geraldo Gonzalez. That is his adopted name."

Lord and ladies, no one in this town was who they say they are. "How do you know this?"

"I know because he was left here with us. We found him twenty years ago, a toddler abandoned on the steps of the convent."

Again, her hope for a clear answer disappeared. "Left by whom?"

"I have no idea. The note with him said he'd been rescued from his mother and needed a new home. We searched for the woman, but when she couldn't be found, we reached out to an older woman in town. She had money, owned apartments, and, at the time, was healthy and active."

That made more sense. Yolanda had seemed a bit old for a son Geraldo's age. "You're saying that the women who have disappeared... this has gone on for decades?"

"Yes. I believe it started with Geraldo's mother, but from then on one or two women a year would go missing."

"Before or after Walid and his people came into the area?"

"Before. Maybe ten years before."

"And the police?"

"They've never solved the crimes or found answers. Although some have tried, including a female mayor who later also went missing."

"But the comandante didn't hesitate to blame Geraldo, even though this had been happening for years."

"Yes. And Geraldo did everything in his power to clear his name from the comandante's accusation. It cost him."

So unfair. "Thank you for sharing Geraldo's secret. Is he aware of his adoption?"

Sister Angelica shook her head. "He used to know, but he seems to have lost this with his head injury."

Dada's skin ran cold. Poor Geraldo. A baby separated from his mother through some horror, maybe murder. And then, when he grew up, separated from another woman, his fiancée, also probably murdered. Bad luck? Or had someone hated his mother enough to torture the man?

Chapter 19

Sion had met a lot of men in his quest to find Sophia that he hated on contact. Men who gave him the creeps or made him feel like beating the *shite* out of them, but he'd never met anyone he detested as completely as Armand Stoker.

The flick, flick of the steel against Armand's dry cuticles echoed across a large, nearly empty room, containing a huge safe, the table he and Sion sat at, and the two guards.

Knowing Armand was good with impatience, hatred, jealousy—any emotion other than happiness which he saw as weakness—Sion sneered at the men by the exit. Though, in truth, their unusual presence had him sweating. "Why the goons?"

Armand, whose crooked nose and caved in cheek told a story, examined his nails, then took steel to them again. "They are here to stop you from leaving."

Sion shifted his gaze again to the guards. Big. But he could take them. Well, he could if they weren't armed. He relaxed his shoulders and tried to keep things light as his mind sorted through ways to get out without getting killed. "What's this about?"

Armand's eyes became slits. "The nun, Sister Dee. You spend a lot of time with her."

Dread snaked over Sion's skin, raising the hair on his arms and neck. The device Dada had given him burned against his pocket. "She's running an art therapy class. She asked me to teach it."

Armand stopped digging at his nails. The room went so quiet, Sion could hear the pounding base from the club downstairs. "You do art?"

Sion glared at the man. "Yeah. That's how I have the skills to do what I do." He raised his hands and flicked them front to back. "Steady hands."

"Does Sister Dee appreciate those steady hands?"

"She's a nun, you daft prick."

"She's a whore!" Armand yelled, slamming his fist onto the table. "And the woman who killed my mother."

Sion grabbed the side of the table in order to keep from flying over it and strangling this man until his foul tongue stopped moving. It took everything in him to sit still and speak. "Sister Dee killed your mother?"

"That was not her name when we lived in French Guiana."

Sion's gut tightened. Dee had mentioned that region, but not her name. What did he know of her?

Enough. He knew enough.

But not her name.

Armand sneered. "Now I have your attention. You didn't know what had crawled into your bed."

Choices, choices. Slam the guy's face into the table a few good times before his goons shot and killed him or get this idiot to talk and figure the rest out later. "Why tell me this?"

"I require your help to trap her."

Fucker. "That's not what I do. I do papers for your boss. That's it." He pointed back at these goons, a taste like vomit lining his throat. "That's what you have these goons for. You don't need me."

Armand shrugged. "Sadly, these are Catholic goons. Now, if I needed them to chop the dick off a priest, no problem, but a nun? They'd sooner harm their own mothers."

Sion didn't buy it. It was more than that. This was punishment. Armand wanted Dee. He thought Sion had had her. He thought both she and Sion belonged to him. Time to press his buttons, then act like the guy had won something. The best way to get Armand to talk.

"How much do I get paid?"

Sion could practically see the drawbridge rolling back up on Armand's mood. Any minute now the guy would call the archers. "I will not pay you, but I will make it simple for you. Your choice is to help me or die here. Tonight."

He had a third choice: get this guy to tell him the plan and then use it to trap him. "What do you need me to do?"

Chapter 20

Dressed all in black, Dada climbed the fire escape. She stopped by Sion's window, pressed on the wood frame, and opened it with a shove. Ducking low, she swung inside.

Dropping her backpack on the floor, she began to pace the dark apartment, her tears as silent as her boots on the pitted wood floor. Armand Stoker was Miles Stoker. Though she'd used a listening device and it had been a fuzzy connection, she knew it was him.

The man had accused her—*her*—of killing his mother. It was unbelievable. And though she knew Sion had played along with Armand, she also worried that Armand's lies had taken her opportunity to tell Sion the truth.

She should have spoken up, spoken her truth when she'd had the chance.

The squeak of the door opening behind her stopped her dead. He must have come straight here.

His distinct gait announced him as he moved across the room to her. She dared not turn. She felt his hands land on her shoulders. Dared not turn. The palms of his hands pressed against her, turning her with a gentle push.

She looked into his face and saw a wash of raw

and tender emotions. He bent and kissed her, full and deep and possessive.

He pulled back, ran a thumb across her wet cheeks. "Your name?"

"Dada Parish."

"Plcase to meet you, Dada," he said, bending to her lips and whispering against them. "Name's Sion Bradford."

She took his lips with her own, moving against them with the same feeling she'd seen in his eyes bubbling inside her.

He began to fiddle with the button on her jacket. "I need to—"

"Yes," she said and let him steer her back toward his bed.

#

"How do you know Armand?"

Tucked in bed with Sion, Dada was ready for the question. And, for the first time in her life, she wanted to tell someone outside her family. "He kept me prisoner as a child. Well, his mother did."

The temperature in the room seemed to change as Sion tensed beside her.

She went on before he could ask. Before she could lose her courage. "My earliest memory of when things started to change was when I was nine. Walking home from a doctor's appointment with my mother, a wealthy man smiled at me. It had been happening a lot of late. I'd grown quickly. So tall. Gangly and thin and uncoordinated. Some men noticed. I remember my mother stopping. I thought she would yell at him, but she introduced me.

"From then on, my mother took me regularly to meet him. He doted on me. I was too young to realize that what he saw in me had nothing to do with me. Nothing at all."

At his silence, she pulled back. Seeing the fearsome look on his face, she ran a hand along his jaw. "I shouldn't be telling you this."

He exhaled a breath that mingled with hers, then braced his hands on her shoulders and drew her closer. "If you see anger in me, it is at myself, for allowing men like Armand to do what they have done. I have been spared enough, luv. Tell me."

She dropped her head onto his shoulder, breathed him in, and allowed herself to go back in time. Back to when her beloved black shoes had been taken from the garbage and her dress was handmade. "My mother explained how I was going to go live with…" She swallowed. She couldn't do it, use his name. "…the Frenchman. I imagined us living in a fine house. Me and her and him. I didn't understand. He already had a family and had arranged for me to be kept by a woman who ran a brothel. Stoker's mother. A slight woman, with a breadth of cruelty—all bitterness and bones—only surpassed by her son. After I was taken—"

"After? Don't skip. I want the details of that day." He shook his head. "Want is the wrong word." He took his hand from her shoulder and rubbed his chest. "I need the details. What do you remember most from that day?"

Closing her eyes again, she leaned her head on the pillow, and took a series of deep breaths that smelled of him. "Mother put every piece of jewelry she owned on me that day. My neck, wrists, on my fingers. The bracelets and rings were so big, they slipped off my wrist and down my fingers.

"I probably looked ridiculous, but I felt so pretty, all excited by the jewelry and fancy clothes made from an old dress of hers. I didn't notice her tension. My first notion that something was wrong was when I saw the man who now calls himself Armand, step out from a truck parked along the city block.

"He was a boy then, a teen, but his eyes were already cruel. They ran up and down my body as he waited for me.

"Before my mother left, she told me, 'Do what the Frenchman says. He will keep you safe if you please him. It is a better life than starving.'"

"Fuck. How could she—"

Dada placed a hand over his mouth. "Don't." Though she knew he only wanted to defend her, she couldn't bear to hear a word spoken against her mother. "My mother was sick, dying from uterine cancer. She thought if she gave me to him, a man who seemed kind, I would at least be educated, fed, taken care of."

"No excuse. She—"

"Shhh." She pressed her fingers to his mouth. "The life she had… She left Suriname during the civil way. She—" She stopped herself, stopped from over-explaining and settled for what she had come to understand. "She could imagine no other choices."

"I'm sorry, luv. So very sorry, but I can't bear to think of you as that child, dressed in your finest, feeling beautiful, only to experience some of the worst the world had to offer."

She brushed a tear from his face. "I have also experienced some of the best the world has to offer."

His eyes dropped to hers. She saw him hesitate, fearful now that he knew part of her truth.

She waited.

He dipped his head, gently kissed her lips. "How long...."

She felt him tense. Heard his heart pounding.

"How long did you live that way?"

"Four years."

"Fuck." He rolled her into his arms, then ran a hand along her back. "How did you get out?"

She breathed in his musk, his warmth, his concern and compassion. "When I first came to be held prisoner, I was conditioned to want and long for… this Frenchman. I was not allowed out of my room. I rarely saw anyone else. I was given the food and gifts he sent or brought to me. By the time he would come, I was desperate for company. He would bring me books, give me lessons. He became everything. Years passed that way. And then I got pregnant."

Sion's breath rushed past her ear. "He stopped coming, didn't he?"

"Yes. But he still he paid for me to be kept."

"So you were left alone in that room?"

Alone? She drew back, angled her head, tried to understand. "No. I wasn't alone. I had my child inside me." She held up the arm with her leather bracelet on it. "I made this for my child from an old hair band. I placed it on my wrist but promised the baby that one day it would be his. I sang and read to him every day. I had never been so bored, and hungry, but so very content."

He ran fingers gently over her bracelet. His mouth tightened. "Hungry?"

"The man you know as Armand was in charge of bringing me food. He was diligent when he knew the Frenchman would come, but when he stopped coming, Armand became sloppy. He stayed away for long days. I believe he was trying to kill me. He wanted my room."

"Luv," Sion choked out. "Please…Come closer."

Hearing his anguish, she put her head back into the crook of his shoulder, let him hold her as tightly as he needed. She rested herself against him, curled into him.

Softly, she said, "I screamed for food sometimes for days. Sometimes he would sit right outside the door laughing as I cried of hunger. I survived only because my room had a bathroom and water."

"Sinister fuck."

"Yes. Until that time, I hadn't sought to escape or rescue myself. It had never crossed my mind. But then I had the child. And we were starving. I began to drop notes from the bathroom window of my prison. Sheer desperation."

"No one saw?"

"Someone did. A boy. He came into the alley every day, picked up my notes, and ran off. I thought he'd bring me food. Help. What I didn't know, what I learned later, was that he'd kept the notes. He stored them in his house."

"He kept them?" Sion's voice was disbelieving and horrified.

"When I went into labor, I cried for help, but no one came. I couldn't understand what was happening to me. A few blocks away, the mother of the boy who had taken and stored my letters, was murdered by her husband.

"The police were called. While investigating, an officer found my letters. He read them. Right then and there. Something in him motivated him to act. Not in a year. Not at the end of the week. Not even when he was done his shift.

"He ran out of the house, down blocks to where my letters told him I was imprisoned. He burst into the home, bullied his way past Armand, raced up the stairs, searched, came to my locked door, broke it down, and found me bleeding to death on the floor.

"Dear God."

"Yes. And on that same day, a day when I should have died, a day when another woman had died, a day when my son also died, I lived. Armand ran away but his mother was arrested. And I was taken to the hospital."

"Oh, luv," Sion's voice was ragged, choked with tears. "A bit more luck than being rescued by a dog. A bloody miracle."

She began to laugh gently, even as the tears rolled from her eyes, down her face to combine with his tears. "That is not the most miraculous part. What happened next delivered me from hell to heaven."

He squeezed her. "Tell me that, because I need to hear the part where you were safe and loved."

Chapter 21

Sion reminded himself again and again that Dada was safe. Safe in his arms. But as many times as he repeated this to himself, he could not let her go. Thankfully, she put up with his embrace.

He kissed away her tears, grateful for her in a way that he thought might make him a fan of God. "What is the miraculous part?"

"That night…"

"The day you were rescued and taken to the hospital?"

"Yes. Later, at night, the police officer who rescued me worked overtime, serving as security for a visiting dignitary, a woman named Mukta Parish. Hoping to impress her, a wealthy woman who championed women's rights, he told her how he'd arrested a man for killing his wife and then had saved a girl held prisoner all in the same day.

"Needless to say, when he told her the story, she was impressed—and curious about the girl he'd saved. So curious that, instead of going to the gala where she was scheduled to speak, she insisted he take her to the hospital to meet me."

Someone walked over Sion's grave, so said the gooseflesh rising across his body. "That's the woman who adopted you, Mukta Parish?"

"Yes. Momma told me when she arrived at the hospital and saw me, gaunt and haunted, it was love at first sight."

Pulling back from her, he ran his hands along her face. Her eyes shone with tears. His heart felt as if it might break. "Can't rightly blame her."

She smiled. "I never believed her. I didn't believe in love at first sight." She brushed aside a tear. "Until, as a love-struck young woman, I saw a man driving down the pitch. And a seed was planted. And then one day, you walked into my life and it bloomed."

"I felt it, luv. Couldn't name it then, but I felt it too. Feel it now."

"I love you, Sion Bradford."

He couldn't breathe for love of her. "I love you too, Dada Parish. I love you."

He kissed her, sweeping his tongue into her soft mouth, possessing and cherishing her with everything he had. The feel of her against him, her warm tongue, sent his head spinning and his heart sprinting. She was his miracle.

He cupped the side of her face. "Must've been odd, walking into your new life."

"I went from the poorest, most base of situations to being adopted by the wealthiest woman in the world. I flew to a home where I was surrounded by love and understanding and healing. A home where I never longed for anything. Well, I longed for one thing, to help free others from situations similar to the one I had endured. And this too, Momma made sure I was given."

"Ah," Sion said, freezing as it all clicked into place. She hadn't been overstating it. It was dangerous what she did. Dangerous in dealing with criminals. Dangerous in being outside the law. "You work for yourself. Your mum. Is that who pays for you to investigate these things?"

"Yes. Not just me. My siblings. And others."

"Okay." She was part of a global vigilante network. Un-bloody-believable. "We have two things going for us with Armand. One, he's a stupid, sadistic bastard. And two, we have backup."

She drew in air with a hiss. "Not really. There are rules against taking certain actions. Things like making assumptions, acting without hard proof, or leaving one case for another. And chasing someone who I have past ties with. All against the rules."

So it was just the two of them.

Grabbing her hand, he put it over his heart. "Do you think it's him? Armand. The one who took Rosa?"

"I do. And I think it's likely he's setting us up. He knows you're not playing along with him."

"I had the same thought when he told me his plan."

"You mean his ridiculous plan to have you drug me and leave me in your car with your car keys? Like that wouldn't end badly for both of us."

"Aye. Tidy way to get rid of you and blame it on me."

"We need a better plan. One that plays to his weakness and anger. Do you have the device?"

"Right. Yes." He reluctantly pulled away from her and searched the floor for his hastily discarded jeans. There. He took the device from his pocket. It looked like a thumb drive. "So what does this do?"

She took it and palmed it. "It copies information from a cell phone or other technology. It has a short range, but you were close enough." She held lifted it. "I can't bring my family in on our plan, but I can get my sister Gracie to use her cyber skills to track where the phone has been. By narrowing down choices, we can hopefully discover where Rosa is being kept."

The unspoken possibility of *if she's being kept* echoed in the air around them.

"And they'll help with this, your family?"

"I might have to call in a favor or two."

"If they won't help," he hated to do this, "we could ask Geraldo."

She put her hand on his arm. "He's done enough."

And this was another reason that he had fallen for her. She cared, even if it could cost her.

#

Because of the nondescript wall behind Sion's bed, Dada sat there with her laptop and sent a text message to her brother Tony—as team leader he'd need to approve Gracie helping locate Rosa.

Transferring Armand's phone records to her computer, she logged into the secure site. Keeping that window open, she searched through Armand's records in a smaller window. The secure site beeped.

"My brother's here," she told Sion, so he'd remember to keep quiet.

Tony came on, black hair askew, blinking and rubbing his hazel eyes. "What's up?"

Had he been sleeping? Dada looked at her clock. "It's 10:30 there."

"Forget what it's like here. I'm teaching lessons tomorrow. Including yours."

A stab of guilt worked its way into her chest. "There's an issue."

"Fill me in."

She paused before answering, something in Armand's text history catching her eye. There was a message from Walid. "A woman," Dada began, trying to let go of the words of the text, "someone I had taken under my wing has gone missing. She left behind her child. I'm worried for her safety."

"You sure she didn't leave her kid?"

Why did everyone assume the woman abandoned her child? "Would I waste your time if she had? Give me some credit."

Her eyes drifted again to the text message of Walid complaining about missing *product.* That was it. How Armand found his women. He stole them from Walid. Walid would not be happy to learn this. Could she could get one snake to eat the other?

Tony grunted what might've been an apology. "Fine. But the point is the same. We're trying to take down a guy who does that to a thousand women a year."

"I believe Walid's head of security, Armand Stoker, kills women for his own pleasure. I found a tomb with at least thirty women buried."

No longer looking the slightest bit tired, Tony leaned toward his monitor. "Shit, D. I'm sorry. You okay?"

"I'm alive, and would like to find this woman before she ends up dead."

"I get it. I do, but you can't divert from an intelligence-gathering mission to find one woman."

"I have a wealth of information on Walid already.

Tonight, I managed to copy information from the cell phone of his head of security."

"Did you transmit it?"

She first needed to make sure Armand had never mentioned her. Her brother would never allow her to risk herself in what he would see as an unexpected and highly emotional situation. "I will. Meanwhile, I'd like your approval to act. A woman's life is in danger."

"Thousands of women's lives are in danger. And you want to take out Walid's head of security?" He shook his head. "Please tell me you're joking. That's not recon. That's straight out attack. We don't want to alert these guys before the actual attack."

He had a point. One she needed to dispel. New plan. "If done right, Walid will never suspect me, but he will need a new head of security."

Tony chewed on that for a minute. "You're saying we could try to get our own person into Walid's organization?"

"Yes. Two birds. One bullet."

"Bullet? You're an okay shot, but you're not Justice."

Insulting, but true. "Yes, but I won't need a bullet." Not now that she had this information anyway. "Armand is stealing from Walid, so what do you think Walid would do if he discovered proof of that? Say, a tomb with thirty women buried."

Tony's eyebrows rose. "If we alert Walid, he'll take this fucker out, leaving us an opportunity to place an operative into his organization."

"*Exactemente*." And instead of planning Armand's murder, she could concentrate on finding Rosa. "So, is it okay to move ahead with my plans?"

Tony's eyes honed in on her. "This can't be a trap, right?"

What? Her mind shifted gears. "I can't see how that would be possible."

"No one's taken notice of you, your mission, or the fact you're helping this woman? No one could be using her disappearance to lure you into anything?"

Her brother was very perceptive, but Rosa hadn't been taken to lure her. That was separate. "Of course not. I'm much too professional for that."

"What about your informant? Does he have a clue?"

Dada's eyes rose to Sion, standing behind the laptop, arms crossed, listening intently. Tony would not understand him. Not. At. All.

"That's a long pause, D. What's going on?"

Dada's ire rose, unexpected and sharp. "I know how to handle an informant." And she did. But Sion wasn't an informant. Not anymore. He was her partner. "Can I have approval for Gracie to get tracking information from the phone?"

Tony snorted. "Transmit it. I'll take a look."

That would take too long. "If you're afraid of Justice—"

"Not only Justice. Momma's nearly as determined to take out Walid, too, so, unless I want to lose my balls—hint, I don't—nothing can risk the mission."

"I'm calling in my favor."

He veered back from the screen, eyebrows shooting to his hairline. "On this? You've been holding that shit over my head for eleven years."

"Which tells you how important this is to me."

Tony rubbed fingers back and forth across his forehead. "You're getting emotional here. This is a mistake."

Although she felt bad and feared risking the mission as much as he did, she'd made a promise to every woman in that tomb. The man who'd hurt them would pay.

"If you think that, if you think any emotional involvement should keep someone from the mission, then what about Justice? She's chasing down the man who murdered her sister. I'm merely looking for a woman who's gone missing."

And trying to take down the man who'd held her captive. But he didn't need to know that.

His hazel eyes closed for a moment. When they opened, they held cold frustration. "I've been blessed with some fucking nut-job sisters."

Chapter 22

After all of the bargaining Dada had done with Tony, Gracie hadn't been able to help out much. Armand's GPS was incomplete, maybe due to occasional jamming. Gracie had been able to use this pattern of jamming to tell her that it was probably close to the restaurant and bar owned by Walid.

Backup plan. Gracie had also been able to use her cyber skills to send Armand a message and make it look like the message had originated with one of the men who worked with him at Walid's. The message was clear—*Walid has found the bodies. He knows you are stealing from him.*

Now, all she had to do was wait for Armand to spook, decide to leave town and gather his belongs, one of which he would consider Rosa.

Seated at the bar, she tensed as Armand, carrying a large leather satchel, neared. She leaned back, *accidentally* bumping him with her arm, securing the tracking device.

Armand looked right at her and cursed, but didn't slow. Shifting the weight of the padding for her disguise, she followed. The extra weight was cumbersome enough to make her exit obvious.

She walked out into the warm night. It was drizzling.

Armand looked back. His eyes swept over her. For all intents and purposes, she appeared to be a heavyset, older man with gray hair, large nose, and stooped shoulders.

Pivoting fast, Armand began walking. Obviously agitated, cursing under his breath, he lit a cigarette.

The sweet smoke hit Dada's nose as she followed. Not a cigarette. All the better. Something stronger to soothe his frazzled nerves.

Keeping track of him on her phone, her heart in her throat, she dropped far enough back that she could only see him through the reflection of a glass window across the street. She kept her distance as he doubled back, practiced surveillance detection, and finally slipped into what appeared to be a corner grocery store that had gone out of business a decade ago.

Fingers flying over the keyboard, she texted Sion the address and told him—*He went inside. Text Walid.*

Shrugging the weight that ached against her shoulders, she inched to the corner and watched.

She couldn't afford to wait for his response. Any delay might cost Rosa her life.

Weapon in hand, she glided around the store with the painted black windows that were a universal signal that someone was hiding something.

Dropping low, the extra weight pressing on her thighs, she squatted beside an HVAC, which was running, and quietly took off her disguise.

She shook out her arms, picked the lock, and swung the door open. Rats scurried across a backroom that had been turned into a makeshift kitchen, with a folding table and some chairs.

She swooped her light over pots and pans that

seemed to have been left mid-dinner rush, along with an electric griddle with grease congealing across it, a series of plastic containers with food and numerous discarded beer bottles.

She lifted her phone from her pocket and glanced at the screen. No Sion. And no signal. Gracie had been right. Armand employed a jamming device.

Dada continued through the door toward the front of the grocery store. Rotten and blackened food in dark refrigerators lined the back wall. A rolling bucket with a mop sticking from the top sat in the middle of an aisle and cans of food covered in dust littered the ground. The Walking Dead had less creepy stores.

There was another door leading to a stairwell—and that door was open. She heard voices and a chain rattling.

Dada crouched, gun raised, and waited. She heard arguing. A woman screamed in terror and pain. Cold fury erupted and Dada rose and entered the door.

A hair-raising scream and then, "Don't touch me, you filthy pig!"

Rosa.

"How's this for a touch?" A slap. "Or this?" Another, louder slap.

Rosa cried out.

Calm and focused, every step weighted and brought down with absolute quiet, she descended. The stairs were dark, enclosed by brick, hiding whatever lay beyond, but a light streamed from around the corner. At the bottom, she took a calming breath and sent a prayer that her abilities would be enough, that she would be quick enough. Gun raised, she pivoted around the corner and slid into the room.

Armand had his back to her, fighting the woman on a floor of bloody, vile mattresses. Rosa. Beaten, chained to a pipe, Rosa fought Armand as he tried to unlock her. This was what had happened to all those women. This was what hatred did.

Dada pointed her gun at Armand. "Leave her."

Armand froze. He dropped Rosa's wrists and turned.

For a moment, she could see Rosa. The young woman stared at her with sunken, tearful eyes. Dada's stomach flipped. Sour bile rose into her mouth.

Armand stepped in front of Rosa, blocking her from view. He smiled, a smile as cold and confident as any Dada had ever seen. "And here is my other whore."

Those words. Something tight rose in her chest. Every breath laced with the metallic odor of blood. Her heart pounded in her ears. "I'll give you to three."

She raised her gun. "One."

Armand rushed at her. "Don't you fucking count at me!"

Everything happened at once.

A sound from behind her, then Rosa screaming, "Behind!" while Armand rushed at her.

Dada shot, hitting him in the chest.

He jerked back and she pivoted.

Then something slammed into the side of her head, knocking her out.

#

Sitting in his car blocks from the bar, Sion gripped his phone, willing it to deliver the information. But something must have gone wrong because the tracker Dada was supposed to put on Armand should have sent the guy's location to his phone.

But nothing.

He'd texted her three times. No response. He punched in her number. His phonc went blank. Dead. This was no coincidence. Someone had messed with his phone. But who and when? Could Dada have tried to protect him…

No. She trusted him as he trusted her. *Bugger.* The thought of Dada facing down a man who had tortured her as a child sent him into a blind panic.

He reached into his cup holder, pulled out the cell that Dada had given him for emergency use only, and dialed the one number she'd programmed into it.

A man answered. "Who the fuck is this?"

"Hi, Tony, mate, this is Juan. Da—" Fuck. "Dee's informant. I need your help."

"What's going on?"

He filled him in. As he spoke, he could hear the man covering the phone, talking to someone else.

"Hold," Tony said, "we're checking her GPS."

Sion pressed the phone to his ear, trying to hear behind the muffled sound.

"I don't fucking care!" Tony yelled to someone. "Fuck protocols. Give me the information."

A split second later, he was back. "Juan?"

"Here."

"Last known has her a dozen blocks from where you are now."

How did he know where he was?

"Her signal winks out. Seems like she went into a building with jamming. I've sent the address."

The phone beeped. Sion looked down, expecting

to have to locate the text message on this unfamiliar phone, but what appeared was a map with a blinking red dot. Sion was that dot. How the fuck?

Sion turned over his car, spun around, and drove.

"Juan?"

Oh, bugger. He put the cell back to his ear. "Got it."

"Do you have a gun?"

Sion's shoulders drew in. "Aye. Dee left one in the glove compartment."

"You don't sound super confident."

"Never shot a gun before."

A pause. "What kind of weapon? I can walk you—"

"No, mate. She's given me instructions before, and you're not going to make me an expert in—" he looked at his phone "—eight minutes. I've got to get to her."

"Call when you have her safe."

He hung up. *Call when you have her safe.* Made it seem inevitable. It felt anything but.

Sion followed the map on the cell, glancing at the glove compartment. Fuck.

Ten minutes later, he parked his car outside an abandoned corner grocery. He reached into the glove box. The weight of the weapon in his hand was immense. He hated guns. Hated the idea of doing to any human body what had been done to his.

Flicking off the safety, he got out of the car. The grocery store wasn't the only abused looking building. Not a lot going on in the neighborhood.

He heard a gunshot. Sion's heart pounded and his feet moved fast around the corner.

He hadn't run full-out run since his injury. He lifted like a madman, cross-trained like a freak, but run? Hurt his soul as much as his leg. Hadn't even been sure those muscles still worked.

Luckily, they did.

He entered the alley behind the store, not as graceful as he'd been—not by a long shot—but still quick. Reaching the open door, he realized he had another problem. He needed to not just be quick, he needed to be quiet. Fucking leg.

#

Vision blurry, head aching, Dada opened her eyes and saw Armand's dead body feet from her. And feet from him, arms drawn around her knees, Rosa sat crying.

She searched for her gun. Something tugged on her leg and clanked. Someone had chained her to the wall. Hands shaking, she grasped the metal and yanked.

"Good. You're awake," a familiar voice said.

Dada rolled. For a moment her heart jumped with excitement. "Geraldo? Thank God!"

Geraldo laughed. "I wouldn't be so quick to thank Him."

His voice. It sounded different. Clear.

"You don't have a brain injury."

"Nope. None."

"You work with Armand."

"Yep."

She saw it then, what her mind and time had not allowed her to see, even when Sister Angelica had come out and told her Geraldo wasn't who he seemed. She'd forgotten the child. "You're his brother."

"Yes. Our mother went to prison after your letters alerted the authorities. My brother ran away with me and came here. You stole my life."

All the pieces fell into place. Armand had never been acting alone. His mother had gone to jail, and he had taken his younger brother and gone to Mexico. He'd given that brother to an older woman, and the whole time had fed him the same poison that was in his mind. He'd made another like himself.

"You killed her," Dada said. "Your fiancée. Comandante Javier had been right."

Geraldo moved from the shadows, holding Dada's gun. "He was getting ready to arrest me, so I made a plan to throw Javier and everyone off the trail. Armand was against it at first because he wanted me to leave the city. But I convinced him it could work." Geraldo tensed, looked over at Armand's body. "I think he enjoyed it, beating me. Nearly killed me, but it worked, and no one questioned me after that. A man who had nearly died looking for his fiancée. Someone with a brain injury who was in the hospital for months recovering."

"You are two monsters," Rosa said and spat on the ground.

He shifted the gun toward her. "The one who lives decides the history, and I see two whores and a dead man who will make a perfect scapegoat."

A whisper of sound came from the stairs as a shadow slipped across the floor.

Geraldo's eyes widened and he spun around.

Sion's blow slammed against his skull.

Geraldo staggered and slipped to his knees. Blood poured from his skull. His face a mask of fury, he rolled onto his back and lifted his gun.

In a boxer's stance, feet shoulder-width apart, broad forearms straight out, head level, balance maintained, Sion directed his gun at Geraldo.

Dada gasped. He wouldn't shoot. He would be shot instead.

With a cry that was part wounded animal and part avenging demon, Sion fired.

The *bam, bam, bam* filled the room. Dada's ears rang. The smell of gunpowder clung to her. She stared in horror as Geraldo grabbed at his stomach, groaning in pain.

Sion slid the weapon Geraldo had dropped away, removed a set of keys hanging from his tool belt, and rushed to Dada.

He put a hand on her face. "Are you okay?"

"Yes. Help Rosa."

After unlocking her, Sion slid over to Rosa. He hissed upon seeing the raw skin under the chain that attached her to the wall. "This might hurt."

"Please hurry and release me," she said, staring at Geraldo, who moaned on the floor.

Blood leaked from his stomach and spread across the cement, joining with the blood of his brother.

Dada knelt at his side, her knees in his blood. "Lift your hands, and let me see the wound."

"Stay away." Geraldo's bloodied hands swung at her. He responded now as was his conditioning—a lifetime of using anger and force—he just expected both to keep working.

But he was harmless in the end.

"You did this to me," Geraldo said. His hands pressed against his wound, sending more blood gushing through his fingers. "Destroyed my… home, my… life. Armand told me the truth. If not for you, the letters, my mother would be alive. And you'd be dead."

Cold washed down her body. "Did you expect me to stay silent? Did you expect me to take the abuse, so that you could go on as you were?"

At her words, Geraldo lashed out with his big, clumsy blood-drenched hands. "I did nothing! It was not me!!"

No. It wasn't. He had been a child when his mother had kept Dada prisoner, but he had learned the same lessons his mother had taught Armand.

Geraldo's fists flailed ineffectively, weapons deprived of their power. Dada felt only pity for him. This dying man who, even now, could not see that his benefitting from a system that had imprisoned her was wrong. To his mind, her refusing to be held prisoner, refusing a life where she was raped, had cost him. That was all that mattered.

Her mind worked over these thoughts, but her eyes skimmed him. He was bleeding out. There was nothing that could be done. And nothing she could say would matter to him, make an ounce of difference. But she could do something, offer something.

Tears streaked his face. He grabbed his bleeding stomach. He cried for his mother, blubbered like an infant denied milk.

Dada placed a hand on his head. This was not her son, but could it have been? They were nearly the same age. If her son had lived and she had died. If her son had been given to Armand. If Armand had brought him here, trained his thoughts, his entitlement, his need to be placed above others, his grievances.

Warped by whatever emotional and physical complexities went into creating a stunted human, but still, this man was human.

And she knew what it was to grow cold on the floor of a building, to feel life slipping away. "Shhh," she soothed. "You are safe. It is okay."

His eyes widened, rolled to her. He saw her. For a moment something clear and defenseless and peaceful filled his eyes. "It hurts," he said.

Closing his eyes, he let out a long breath and went silent.

Chapter 23

Back in her room at the convent, aching head propped on a pillow against her headboard, Dada stared into her brother's eyes. He was seated on a wooden chair by her bed, looking agitated and worried.

Worried enough that, after a call from Sion, he had arranged to come to Mexico.

"I'm pulling you out," Tony said.

Shaking her head caused Dada's stomach to turn. She pressed the bandage covering her head wound. "You're overreacting."

"The fuck I am. Your cover is blown."

"No, it's not. Juan covered for me, and he told the police that he'd followed Geraldo because he'd been acting suspiciously. He even covered for Walid, earning him an in with the man. We have more access to the traffickers now than before."

"I don't give a shit about how you covered your tracks. I fucking asked you if someone could be setting a trap."

"There was no way to tell—"

"Bullshit. You missed it. Geraldo set you up. He gave Juan the coordinates, right? That's what you said."

She leaned forward, lifting her head and shoulders enough that the pillow slipped down, wedged against her lower back. "Yes. It appears he tried to kill Juan and me."

"Appears? Geraldo led you in there, set off the explosion. Figures he'll wait a couple days for you two to be noticed missing. And then boo-hoo to the cops about how he'd given Juan some directions, because good ol' Juan was looking into the disappearance of his fiancée. Geraldo couldn't have asked for a better scenario. He gets you and Juan out of the way, exposes the tomb, which gets rid of Armand, then takes control of Oaxaca, and is cleared for the tragic disappearance of his fiancée."

"It's a mistake anyone could have made. I did a thousand things right, and I won't have you harp on my one mistake."

Tony dragged a hand down his face. "All it takes is one, D. That's it. One. You and Justice are going to be the death of me."

"I'm not like Justice."

Tony exhaled, and rolled his head around on his neck. "You're more like her than you think. If you weren't, you'd leave. We've done everything you asked. We took that woman you were concerned about, Rosa, and flew her and her son Carlos to relatives in Canada. You did good. Let us put someone from another unit out here."

"No. I'm here until this is done."

Tony's eyelids lowered with suspicion. "Is this about your informant, this Juan guy?"

"I don't know what you mean."

Tony snorted. "First, he looks nothing like a Juan."

Dada shook her head. "Trust me when I tell you no one in this town uses their own name."

"Second, I don't like the way he looks at you."

Dada wasn't going anywhere near that minefield. Fishing her pillow out, she placed it behind her head, leaned back, and hoped Tony didn't notice her ignoring that question.

But Tony wasn't one for tiptoeing past a subject. "He looks at you like you're sleeping together. And he'd give his right ball to see that kept happening."

"That's none of your concern."

"Fuck. You kiddin' me, D?"

"I'm handling this."

"I'm pulling you."

No. No way. A lifetime for her and Sion started now. "No. You aren't."

"The hell—

"You need me. More importantly you need Juan. He still has an in with Walid."

That stopped him. He waited a beat. "An in how?"

"He supplies the man with…" she shrugged, "physical entertainers."

"What, like jugglers."

"Like men more than willing to hurt each other and have sex in front of Walid while they do it."

Tony's winced. "Momma won't approve this."

"So don't tell her."

"D—"

"Juan is doing this for us, and I'm not using or manipulating him. He is doing this for me, for these women, so we will help him find Sophia."

Tony stood, strode across the room, and punched the stone wall. "Fuck."

He shook out his hand and turned to her. "This is

the last near-death experience you get. Next time, I pull you."

Dada did not envy him his position as team leader on this mission. She put her arms out for him. He came over and embraced her.

"Just be careful. I don't want to lose you," he said into her hair.

"You won't. No one is going to die on this mission."

"Oh yeah? We're that good?"

"Yes. We are. And I'm just that lucky."

Chapter 24

Darkness soaked into Sion's bones and sweet exhaustion weighted his legs. He longed for a few more moments holding Dada, but knew she wanted to help more in the soup kitchen—especially now that she spent so many nights with him.

He ran a hand over her arm. "Give me a minute." He pulled her closer. "You in my arms… It's precious. Not to be rushed. One more breath, one more inhale of your sweet skin, before you have to leave. That's what I need."

He meant it. Things had gotten better after finding Rosa, but it wasn't over. It wouldn't be until Justice, Dada's sister, was able to put an end to Walid. So once Dada got out of bed, the threats out there, the danger, the pressure of dealing with Walid and his new man, sifting through Armand's files to locate Sophia, all of that returned. "A minute, luv, a minute more."

She sighed and rolled closer to him. "I have to go. And with barely two hours' sleep."

He grinned, remembering how she'd coaxed him from sleep two hours ago. He'd woken, moaning and throbbing, to find she had his dick in her mouth. "Hottest thing I've ever awaken to."

She laughed, pushed away with a regretful sigh, and stepped fully out of bed.

He watched her cross the room. Beautiful. "You've perfected walking away, luv." She shook her bottom, and he flat out died. "You're torturing me."

Laughing evilly, the sexy witch, she closed the bathroom door.

He relaxed into the pillow and drifted off thinking of her, the best wake-up call of his life.

Dada screamed. Bloodcurdling. He threw himself out of bed and charged into the bathroom to find her perched on the edge of the tub. She pointed down.

What the bloody hell—

He started to laugh. "Really, luv? It's a spider."

"A spider the size of my foot. I've incapacitated it. Take it outside."

Incapacitated? The spider, if that's what it was, didn't move. Ach, she'd hit it with his shaving gel. Not dead but, as she said, but woozy.

He bent down. It definitely wasn't average size. Opening the cabinet, he pulled out a piece of cardboard from a shoebox and slid it under the spider's heavy body.

He maneuvered the monstrosity out of the bathroom, through the room, and onto the fire escape. He shut the window. Locked it. Could never be too certain.

Returning, he found his woman still holding the shower curtain rod. Had to admit that was exactly where he'd wanted her. He shut the door behind him.

"There's a lovely." He crooked his finger at her. "Need some comforting?"

With as much class as he'd come to expect from her, she climbed down from the tub, walked forward, and slammed into him. Fast and hard.

Which made him hard. Fast.

He wrapped his arms around her as she began to kiss his chest and rub him with hands that shook. Nothing got the motor going quicker than a near-death experience.

His body responded in a way that was all about keeping her safe and taking her here and now. His hands grasped her arse with a grip that intended to do both. Kissing her with as much reassurance as he could convey, he lifted her onto the sink.

Her soft lips clung to his. Her hands dragged at him. Her legs wrapped around him so tightly, she pushed him toward her opening. Wet, soaked, and ready.

He thrust into her softness, and she moaned and mewled, a soft needful sound. She was doing him in with those sounds.

He pumped into her, took her with every bit of need and want, the power of his thrust speaking for his heart.

She cried out, whimpering and moaning, writhing and rocking, and then biting his shoulder as she came. He rode into her, ignoring the *bang, bang, bang* of his knees against the cabinet doors, toppling over the edge with her.

Spent, he buried his head in her shoulder. "I love you."

She brought her mouth to his ear. "I love you more."

Epilogue

Dressed in heels and a dress that clung to her in a way she knew would please Sion, Dada climbed the stairs to his new apartment.

Dada detested the time away from Sion, her man, but as a member of the League of Warrior Women, she was required to go home, make reports, and allow herself to take part in the final arrangements for taking out Walid and his brother Aamir.

Things were progressing nicely. Well, except for her sister's insistence on killing both the men at the same time. That was foolish, but Momma had approved of Justice's plan, and who was Dada to say anything?

It wasn't much longer now. Mere weeks. Soon, she and Sion would be free to live wherever they wanted.

She climbed the steps to Sion's apartment, happy to be home. And not sure when she'd begun to think of him as home. But that's the way it was. It wasn't his apartment—though they had been living together now for nearly a year—it was him.

The smell of dinner seeped under the door as she placed her key in the door. He had music on. A salsa. And was dancing at the stove with an apron wrapped around him. His body swayed as he added a pinch of spice to what smelled like *pozole*. Yum. She was ravenous.

And not just for food. She was ravenous—starved—for him. The moment he began to twerk at the stove, she knew he was aware of her.

Smiling, she put her bags down and walked across the room. Her hot hands slid under the thin material of his apron to his toned, hard abs. He didn't stop moving his hips, only bumped them back against her, sending desire flying through her.

She bit his ear. "Take this off. I need you."

After he turned off the burner, he spun in her arms. And without a word, he was kissing her, claiming her, welcoming her home.

Her heart felt whole again as the blood began to pound through her body. And she realized, she'd do anything to keep him safe.

So she told him, whispering in soft Spanish, "*Querido, eres mi mundo*."

His lips covered hers, silencing her, telling her with his body what she'd said with her words. She was his world, too.

She let herself sink into the feeling. For now, all was as it should be.

#

Good food, good sex, and now the promise of this mission finally coming to an end.

A few weeks left, and her family would take out the men who were holding thousands of women around the world, including Sophia, captive.

It was as good a day as any day he was with her. Now, he sat in a striped chair on the balcony with his woman half-dressed in his lap, afraid to hope what she'd just told him was real.

Sophia's alive. She's safe.

"Say it again, luv. Please."

Dada squirmed in his lap, turned to face him. Behind her, the city glowed pink with the sunset. "She's alive, my love. She's safe. Rescued from a slaver."

"Sophia's alive?"

"Yes. We couldn't find her because the trafficker had called her by a different name. Cookie."

"When can I see her?"

Dada smiled, put her hands on his face. "You can head to the States—to safety—tomorrow."

Sion's mouth set into a grim line. This wasn't the first time she'd tried to get him to give up this mission and leave it to her. "No, luv. I'm in this with you. If she's safe, I will see her again." And he would. He longed to see Sophia, see for himself that the child—no longer so young or innocent—was safe. But he trusted Dada and her family. If they had her, she was safe.

"But—"

This woman. "I leave here when this mission is done." He placed his hand on her stomach and rubbed. "I leave here when you and our son leave here. Not a moment sooner."

She smiled against his lips and kissed him. "Not much longer, my love. And until then, we have glorious Mexican sunsets, good friends, and hot nights to enjoy."

Speaking of hot nights… He stood, lifting her into his arms.

She cried out, laughing. "Your leg! You can't possibly carry me!"

Oh yes he could. And would. "My wife and son are always safe in my arms, luv. Trust me."

She quieted and whispered, "Forever, my love. Forever."

Acknowledgements

I'd like to thank my editor and one of my dearest friends, Terri-Lynn DeFino. Your incredible talent and insights helped transform this manuscript, making it so much more than it would have been without you. More than that, I want to thank you for being here for me as I venture into this world of self-publishing. Your love of this project, your support and belief in it, not only transformed this work, it has helped to shape and transform me into a better writer.

I'd like to thank Daniel Ladinsky for allowing me to use part of his translation of St. Catherine's poem from his marvelous book *Love Poems From God: Twelve Sacred Voices from the East and West*.

And thanks, as always, to my agent Michelle Grajkowski for her encouragement, help, and support.

A huge Thank You to my copy editor and production editor, Judi Fennell. I sincerely appreciate all of your hard work and advice as I've navigated this self-publishing process.

To my incredible cover designer, Richard Lamb, I can't thank you enough for your incredible artistic talent. You managed to create a gorgeous cover that captured my story and my heart.

Finally, a big thank you to all the hard-working and supportive people at Sourcebooks. It is thanks to you that the Black Ops Confidential series is out in the world, and I couldn't appreciate and love you more.

About the Author

Diana Muñoz Stewart is the award-winning romantic suspense author of the upcoming Bad Legacy series and the current Black Ops Confidential series, which includes *I Am Justice, The Price of Grace, and The Cost of Honor* (Sourcebooks). She lives in eastern Pennsylvania in an often chaotic and always welcoming home that—depending on the day—can include a husband, kids, extended family, friends, and a canine or two.

When not writing, Diana can be found kayaking, doing sprints up her long driveway—harder than it sounds—practicing yoga on her deck, or hiking with the man who's had her heart since they were teens.

Sign up for Diana's newsletter to receive free content related to this series and be informed of her next release!

https://dianamunozstewart.com/newsletter/

CPSIA information can be obtained
at www.ICGtesting.com
Printed in the USA
LVHW081303101121
702972LV00011B/297

9 781951 467012